I0673045

THE

PROTECTORS

T. N. SIMMONS

THE PROTECTORS

Copyright © 2017 by T.N. SIMMONS

All rights reserved. Printed in the United States of America. No part of this book may be used or reproduced in any manner whatsoever without written permission except in the case of brief quotations em- bodied in critical articles or reviews.

This book is a work of fiction. Names, characters, businesses, organiza- tions, places, events and incidents either are the product of the author's imagination or are used fictitiously. Any resemblance to actual persons, living or dead, events, or locales is entirely coincidental.

For information contact :

TERRICANSIMMONS@GMAIL.COM

http://m.facebook.com/TerricaNicoleSimmons/

Book Formatting template by Derek Murphy @Creativindie

Book and Cover design by Les Solot

Book Editing by A.J. Myers and Staci Troilo

About the Author photo by Carissa Campbell

ISBN: 978-0-692-98047-7

First Edition: November 2017

TABLE OF CONTENTS

DEDICATION

This, my very first book, is dedicated to my husband, Logan Simmons and to my favorite author AJ Myers, for always believing in me and giving me encouragement along the way. My amazing children, Aiden, Peyton and Evelyn for always encouraging me even when they had to eat take out another night because I was writing. 😊 My mother Lynn Price for loving me unconditionally and to Shaun Lovett for his love of teaching taekwondo to my children. May you rest in peace my sweet friend.

Chapter One
ON MY OWN

The frigid night air whirls around my face in the dark alley. The flickering streetlight makes it difficult to see as I try to reach the road. I speed up my pace, and my heart starts pounding faster as though it may explode at any moment. I jump at the sound of metal hitting the ground. I can't bring myself to turn around.

Fear has taken control of my body, and I cannot run nor scream. I stand completely frozen, perspiration building on my forehead, then I hear footsteps coming toward me. I must force myself to move. I gain control of my legs and manage one slow, unsteady step. Then another. And another. My momentum builds, and I break into a run. Only then do I turn around...and see him in shadows, hiding his face as he sends a wave of flames rushing towards me.

Just before the flames engulfed my body, I woke with a start, soaked with sweat and trembling. I reminded myself once again it was just a dream. It was always the same dream, haunting me throughout the night.

Most people hated mornings, but I was glad to greet the day and put the night behind me.

After my shower, I wiped the steam from the mirror and stared at my reflection. My cheeks were pink from the heat of the water, and my jade eyes were streaked with red from lack of sleep. I wondered if I looked like my mother. Did I have her wide smile or her curly red hair? Would she recognize me?

I forced myself to smile at the weary-eyed creature staring back at me through the looking glass and promised her, "Today is going to be a good day." I repeated the sentence several times to myself. Today is the day I will finally begin my search for my parents.

After a quick blow-dry, I threw on a pair of jeans and my favorite black sweater. I took one last look in the mirror before I headed downstairs to meet my taxi. My eyes now shone with optimism and my smile beamed confidence. I was ready. One more time, I repeated my mantra. "Today is going to be a good day."

I took a deep breath, fully expanding my lungs. My mind was clear and full of possibilities. I had waited eighteen years for this blissful feeling of freedom. No more bouncing from foster home to foster home. No more hiding in closets, scared of who may sneak in during the night.

My hands trembled as I unfolded the paper holding the address to the convent. Today perhaps I would find out who I was and where I was from. Would anyone there remember the day I was left at the door?

"2215 Monroe Ave, please," I said to the taxi driver.

He gave me a questionable look in the rearview mirror. "Miss, that's over an hour away. Are you sure you don't want to save some money and take the bus?"

"Yup, I'm sure."

He shrugged, started the meter, and pulled into traffic. The ride was quiet, which was nice, but my nerves were still on edge. We passed a large museum to my left and I watched the crowd of tourist snap family photos. Perhaps one day I would have that same luxury.

"Would you like me to wait, miss?" My driver asked as we pulled up and parallel parked along the street in front of the building.

"Yes, please." I climbed out of the cab and looked up at the massive convent. This was it. I was finally there. A ball of nerves began to tingle in my stomach.

The building was tall and outlined in large grey-and-brown stone. It was beautiful and reminded me of a medieval style castle. There was also something very sad and lonely about the old place. Twenty-five stairs led up to the massive door, above which was a carved sign reading, "Heavenly Angels Convent".

I opened the large door and walked inside. The room was lightly lit with candles placed along the entrance ways and up the stairs, giving it a glowing effect. It was sparsely decorated, making it easier to navigate to where I needed to go. I walked up to small desk and rang the silver bell for service. An older lady wearing a black habit and white veil approached.

"May I help you?" She donned a small pair of eye glasses, looked up at me, and squinted as if she was trying to figure out who I was. She adjusted her glasses to get a closer look and whispered something I couldn't quite make out.

"Yes ma'am, I am hoping you might be able to assist me." I rolled my sweaty hands together. "I was dropped off here as an infant eighteen years ago. I am trying to locate records or witnesses... any information that might help me in my quest to find my birth family."

She stepped forward, and gave me a good look. "Ah, yes, I remember you. My name is Sister Ann Marie, and I've been here over twenty years now. I remember you like it was yesterday. Your name is Jaime Weaver. When you came here, you were so tiny. Only about a week or two old. Your mother stopped by, said she was in some trouble, and asked if you could stay here until she returned. She gave a large donation to the convent to provide everything we needed to care for you. Of course, we were more than happy to help.

"We enjoyed you so much that we lost track of time. Month after month went by with no word from your mother. You were about five months old when we got a package in the mail saying that if we received it, then your mother and father had passed away. The instructions were to call social services and to give them the enclosed paperwork containing your first name only. The other items were to be sent to a post office box in your full name, and we were to hold the key until you one day found your way back to us.

"Our hearts were broken to see you placed in the system, but we gave our word to do as your mother asked. Social services came to claim you right away. We didn't even have time to say goodbye."

I saw a tear run down her cheek as she looked up at me and touched my chin. My heart went out to her as her loss was also my own. Why would my parents want me in the system when I was obviously loved at the convent?

"I tried to find you some years later, but failed with every attempt. You look so much like your mother, you know." She smiled and opened a drawer in the desk. "I am the only one left from those days. Other than you, of course."

After rummaging around in the drawer for a few moments, she handed me a piece of paper with an address and a gold necklace with a key attached. The chain was long and could easily slip over my head. The little silver key had a square handle that displayed the number 501.

"I hope you find the answers you are looking for, dear. You will always have a place here should you need it." Sister Ann Marie gave me a tender hug.

I hugged her back, saddened to have to leave so soon even though I had only just met her. I was usually uncomfortable with physical gestures, but with her if felt natural. Maybe that was how a child felt when they hugged a grandparent.

"Please keep in touch, sweet Jaime," she whispered as she walked me to the door.

Dazed as I literally held the key to my existence in my hand, I returned to my cab. My stomach was full of butterflies, and my heart was heavy knowing I would never get the chance to meet my parents.

"To the post office, 3115 Ryder Street, please," I said to my driver as I buckled my seatbelt. "I am sorry to keep you waiting so long. I know it's your job, but I appreciate all you are doing."

He looked up at me and smiled then, typed in the address into his navigation device. He'd removed his hat, revealing his sandy blond hair. His voice was cheerful when he said, "I've never had anyone thank me before. You are very welcome, miss. My name is Troy, by the way."

"Pleased to meet you, Troy. My name is Jai."

We gave each other a smile and began our journey to the post office. It wasn't far, maybe a block or two from the convent. I smiled and got out of the car, clutching my key tightly in my hand.

I walked into the post office and went toward the back. The building was small, and numbered boxes lined one wall. I suddenly felt nervous and claustrophobic in the small space. I found the box corresponding to the number on my key—501. I took a deep breath, inserted the key, and opened the door.

Inside was an eight-by-ten size silver box with gold flowers etched on the top. The box was sealed and didn't appear to have a lock. I had no idea how I was going to get the thing open, but I decided I would worry about that when I got home. At that moment, all I really wanted to do was get out of that tiny little post office.

Once back in the cab, I asked Troy to take me home. My mind raced, and my heart fluttered with excitement as I gripped the mysterious box in my arms. When we arrived at my apartment, I paid Troy, adding a nice tip for his patience with me, and thanked him once again for his time.

I dug around in my pocket for my keys. My hands trembled with anticipation as I tried to unlock the door. I juggled my new inheritance, trying not to drop it in the process of getting in the door. I was anxious to get inside, anxious to find a way to open that box and see what my parents had left me.

Looking back, even I couldn't have expected what I would find or the way it would change my life forever.

Chapter Two

THE BOX

I walked into my tiny one-bedroom apartment and sat down on my brown futon to inspect my unusual inheritance. It was sealed tight, and I couldn't force it open with only my fingers. I grabbed a butter knife out of my kitchen drawer and attempted to pry it open, but the only thing I managed to do was bend my knife.

I didn't want to break the box, but I was desperate to see its contents. Perhaps a blow torch would work. In the heat of frustration, I threw it on the ground in hopes that it would crack open. Nothing happened.

Other than a loud bang, the results were the same as my bent butter knife—the mysterious box remained firmly, and infuriatingly, shut tight.

***

After two days of searching for a way to open the box—using some very creative methods along the way, I might add—I was beginning to lose hope. Frustrated and disappointed, but not defeated, I placed the box on my nightstand while I put on my work uniform—a blue shirt and a pair of khaki pants.

My job at Walmart selling fishing and hunting supplies was easy but extremely boring. I often wished I worked at the front cash registers. They were always busy.

When my taxi showed up, I was glad to see that Troy wasn't my driver. I didn't feel much in the mood to talk. I couldn't get that blasted box out of my head and cursed my unknown parents for not leaving me instructions.

I arrived at work fifteen minutes early, as usual. Krista nearly knocked me over with a football-tackle-style hug when she saw me.

"Krista, it's so good to see you! I have so much to tell you," I said as we released our embrace. Krista was one of the most beautiful women I had ever met, and I loved her, from her long raven hair to her perfectly-painted toes. Her hourglass figure and her emerald eyes paired with her dark hair made her look like a goddess.

"I have missed you the last few days. Where have you been, little lady?" She shook her pointy finger at me.

"That's a long story I would love to talk about over dinner at my house. If you're up to it?"

"Absolutely, but only if you're making your killer mac and cheese." She fluttered her eyelashes at me and I laughed.

I'd never had a steady family, but I'd been friends with Krista since I was fourteen. We were more like sisters, really. She was the only constant in my life. Foster homes came and went, but she was always there for me.

We started working at the local Walmart when we turned sixteen. Neither of us could afford college, so we decided we would begin working early and save up enough money to start a new life that didn't include caseworkers and juvenile courts.

I had saved up more than three thousand dollars when I accidentally left my checkbook ledger open. My foster parents took almost every dime I'd managed to save, claiming it was owed to them for my room and board— as if they didn't already get a check from the state for that and weekly 'rent' payments every Friday when I cashed my paycheck. After that, I gave my earnings to Krista to hold for me until my birthday last July, since her money went into a special account only she and I knew about.

Krista and I had plans to share an apartment, but she was still six months away from her eighteenth birthday. So, for the last three months, I'd been on my own. I had enough money saved and with two years of employment it was easy to get a small rental contract.

I managed to scare the crap out of my customer when I screamed because one mischievous cricket jumped out of the bucket on to my hand. Those things seriously creep me out. The rest of my shift was uneventful. I clocked out and told Krista to meet me in an hour.

***

The doorbell rang, and I heard Krista yelling for me to hurry and open the door. She was early, and I was still cooking. I rushed so I didn't burn our dinner. She was disheveled, out of breath, and appeared to have been running.

"Why on earth are you screaming?"

"There is a super-hot guy on his way up the elevator, and I am a hot mess. He can't see me like this!" I rolled my eyes at her and we both busted out laughing.

"Seriously, we need to get you a boyfriend," I teased and tousled her hair as she stared at her reflection in the mirror and smoothed out her shirt until it was perfect again.

"You're one to talk. When is the last time you had a boyfriend, when you were six?" She stole a large bite of un-melted cheese out of the pot.

I finished preparing the pasta while Krista proceeded to tame her new troll hairstyle in my tiny bathroom mirror.

Apparently satisfied she no longer looked like she stuck her finger in a light socket, Krista came in and helped set two places for us at my small round kitchen table. As soon as I placed the pasta on the table, she dug in as if she hadn't eaten in a year.

"This is so good." She shoveled the creamy noodles into her mouth. "I can't get enough of your macaroni and cheese. It's so much better than my mom's."

"Well, it's not hard to make, but you better not tell Momma Jane that. She won't cook for me ever again." I laughed.

Krista's mom, Jane, owned a local catering company and was an amazing cook. I grew up calling her Momma Jane because she was the closest thing to a real mother I ever knew. She told me she would always be my Momma Jane, no matter what, and the name stuck from that day forward.

Krista and I ate, and then I showed her my special locked box and asked if she had any ideas about how to open it. She attempted to pick the lock with her bobby pin and she bent her debit card when she tried to slide it through the sealed lid.

Nothing worked. Even Krista's magic lock-picking skills didn't get the stubborn thing to open. It was starting to really frustrate me. So, when Krista said goodnight and headed home, I decided what I really needed was a night out. The dance club was only a block away from my apartment and the street was brightly lit at night. I liked to listen to the music and be around other people for a while. Even if I didn't know a single person there.

I put on a low-cut green dress that fit my body like a glove and ended just above my knees. I slipped on a pair of white strappy high heels and gave my hair a once over. Satisfied with my party girl ensemble, I smiled. I looked hot in my dress. I snapped a few selfies and sent them to Krista as I locked my door and headed outside.

I arrived just after eleven. The club was slow for a Friday night. The bartender, a much older gentleman, skillfully and quickly served multiple drinks at a time, careful to check for the notorious red X—the mark of the underaged –for those ordering alcoholic beverages. I found an empty seat at the bar and ordered an unsweetened tea. There was a live band playing on the stage, and I turned to listen while the bartender fixed my drink.

The lead singer had blond spiked hair with red tips and was wearing a pair of ripped up leather pants and a jean jacket with the word "fireball" written in red across the back. I assumed he would be singing a heavy metal song. To my surprise, the band started singing songs from multiple eras and styles. I could feel the bass booming throughout my body, almost like an unnatural heartbeat.

I'm not much of a dancer, but that night I felt free. So much had happened in the last week since I moved out on my own. I walked out on the raised dance floor and started swaying with the music. The lights above me blinked assorted colors as they moved around the room. It felt so good to let loose. I danced song after song, not caring what I looked like or who was watching. In that moment, I was just me.

The band stopped playing for a small break, so I went to get another tea from the bar. The bartender brushed his hand through his silver hair and smiled at me.

"Unsweetened tea?" he asked.

"Yes, please." I smiled at him. "You have a wonderful memory, sir."

"It comes with practice. Enjoy." He smiled then went back to work.

"Well, hello there, miss."

I turned around to see Troy standing there, smiling. He looked handsome in his whitewashed jeans and form-fitting blue t-shirt. He had a beer in one hand and a mixed drink in the other. He attempted to pass the fruity mixed drink to me until he spotted my fashionable red X, then he quickly pulled the drink away.

"It's Jai, and it's good to see you." I replied.

"Are you here alone?" he asked.

"Yup. I don't have many friends." I took a sip of my tea.

"Well, then would you like to be my friend, Miss Jai?" he said with a very charming southern voice as he grabbed my hand and placed a kiss on it.

I laughed and replied in the best southern belle voice I could muster up. "I would be delighted to be considered your friend, Mr. Troy."

We both laughed. He asked me to dance, and I accepted. I just didn't want him to get the wrong idea. I didn't see him as boyfriend material for me. He was more Krista's type. We danced to a few more songs before I decided it was time to call it a night.

"Would you like me to walk you home?" he asked.

"That would be very kind of you."

We walked along the street to my apartment, laughing at silly jokes and talking about cheesy pickup lines. The night was clear, allowing the stars to light up the sky above us. His company was easy, and I could tell we were going to be great friends.

"Thanks for walking me home." I gave Troy a quick hug while keeping a little distance between us.

"Anytime." Then he turned to walk back to the club.

I walked into my tiny one-bedroom apartment and threw on some comfortable flannel pajamas and a baggy tank top while thinking about how much fun I had at the club. Putting my matchmaker brain to work, I wondered if Krista and Troy would make a good couple.

Soon my attention turned back to my conundrum. I picked up my puzzling box and shook it to hear its unknown contents. Still with no idea how to open it, I placed it on my bedside table before I crawled into bed. My head was filled with questions of my parents as I dozed off.

I woke from my normal reoccurring nightmare, sweaty and nervous. When I sat up in the bed, the first thing I saw was that blasted box—taunting me. What If the stupid thing held the secret to why I've had the same stinking nightmare every night for as long as I can remember? I picked it up and looked at it, and it suddenly made me furious.

"Why won't you open?" I screamed, and slapped the top of it.

At my touch, the box let off a faint glow. Unsure what I had done, I touched it again. This time there was no glow. I knew I wasn't crazy. I knew what I saw. True, I might have still been half asleep, but there had been no mistaking that glow. I sat there, frustrated, and tried to remember exactly what I had done the first time. I had touched it, and then I had screamed at it...

I had screamed at it to open.

Figuring I was crazy, I decided to give it a try. My palms were sweaty, but I laid my hand on top of the box again. As I was holding my breath, my voice came out as barely a whisper.

"Please open for me?"

The next thing I saw, the flowers started to move, and the box began to vibrate, and it opened. What in the world just happened? It couldn't be real. I pinched myself, and a tiny yelp escaped my lips at the sting. I wasn't dreaming. My stomach tickled, and my heart skipped a beat.

I looked inside the box and found pictures, letters, a birth certificate, and a bracelet with the initials JGW. I looked at the photos first. There was one of my mom and dad on their wedding day. My mother's long amber hair was in curls down her back, accenting the beautiful lace-lined white dress. She was smiling at my father, and her smile was stunning. My father had dark hair which accentuated his black suit. He was so handsome, and his eyes were fixed on his lovely bride. There was no doubt they were in love.

There were several pictures of her pregnant and one of the two of them holding me. They were staring down at me, both holding my hand. I could see their love for me in their expressions. Tears escaped my eyes and rolled down my cheeks. I dried my eyes and opened the letter.

My dearest Jaime Grace Weaver,

First and foremost, I want you to know your father and I love you so very much. We had to keep you safe. This is going to sound very strange to you, but I need you to understand it is all true and your life is about to change in ways you never imagined. I'm so sorry you are having to learn about this in a letter, but the odds were not in our favor. Something happened the day you were born. There was a cosmic shift that created an extremely large amount of energy. I was wearing the amulet of Aether, the fifth element, and somehow the amulet merged with you. It set off a red flag to every dark creature within a hundred-mile radius.

We ran for days but feared they were gaining too much ground. With no more places to hide, we were forced to bind you from using your powers. We took you to the convent to keep you hidden. Obviously, if you are reading this, we didn't make it back for you.

You will soon find out that you possess certain abilities that will be difficult to control. You should have been in training for years, but the only way we could keep you hidden was to bind you. There are others out there who want to use you for these powers. This will prove a most arduous process for you, and I am so sorry we are not there to see you through it.

We pray for the day you will free us. The enclosed bracelet will be your most valuable key to finding us. Keep it close to you always. We love you with all our heart. Please be safe, my sweet girl.

Until we meet again.

Your loving mother and father,

Roberta and Jimmy Weaver.

Chapter Three

SECRETS

Until we meet again. The sentence kept circulating through my head over and over. They are alive. My parents are alive!

I frantically started searching through the maps for any clue of where they could be. None of them made sense. The maps looked like they were drawn in the 1800s. I sighed and opened the book to find strange symbols and chants written on the pages.

Witchcraft? Were my parent's witches? That couldn't be true. There was no such thing as magic. Maybe they were locked up in an institution somewhere. At least I had their names to aid in my search to locate them.

I just couldn't get the idea out of my head that there was much more to this story. I wasn't even sure I was ready to find out anymore. I had been hoping for a normal life. Finding out I might possibly be insane by birthright didn't quite fit my plans.

I looked over at the clock. It was two in the morning, and I really needed to get some rest. I packed everything except the bracelet back into the box. If by chance this was all true and someone was looking for me, then I needed to keep it hidden. I stood up on my bed and removed one of the ceiling tiles, slid the box in, and replaced the tile.

"There, not my first rodeo keeping secrets." Then I placed the bracelet on my wrist. It fit perfectly.

My head was heavy, and a yawn escaped my mouth. I turned the light off, fluffed my pillow, and slipped off into a deep sleep.

***

I woke feeling well rested considering the night's events. I dressed in my usual work clothes and called my trusty new friend Troy the Taxi Driver for my daily ride to work.

"You look different today," Troy stated as he turned to watch me slip into the backseat.

"I guess I just got some much-needed rest," I replied, not wanting to elaborate on my new-found information.

***

It was a perfectly normal day, but it seemed to be dragging by abnormally slow. I was starting to think it was never going to end when my relief arrived, and I was allowed to escape. Troy was right on time for my pick up, and I was grateful.

"Hello, Jai, how was your day?" he asked.

I climbed into the yellow taxi. "Boring, but productive nonetheless. How about your day?"

"Eh, it was work. Nothing exciting." He looked nervously at me. "Would you like to go to the club tonight? Not as a date or anything, just thought it would be fun."

"I'd love to go," I said, as I winked at him. "My friend, Krista, will be with me. I think you're going to love her."

He dropped me off at my usual location, and we said our goodbyes. I called Krista to ask her to come over in about an hour, but she was already on her way.

Krista arrived about thirty minutes later, and we went over outfits and hairstyles for what seemed like hours before we finally settled on what to wear. I slipped on a denim mini skirt and a silver strappy backless top. Krista, a little bolder, decided on a tight, low-cut, little black dress. She was dressed to impress, for sure.

Once our hair and makeup were perfect, we headed out the door—after taking about half a million selfies first, of course. Troy met us at the entrance to my apartment. He looked great. His brown sweater and khaki pants paired well with his hazel eyes and dirty blond hair. He was handsome, and I saw Krista blush as she glanced at him several times while we walked to Alan's dance club.

The club was packed. A new band was playing, and a lot of out-of-towners were there for the show. We practically had to push our way to the bar, and then stand there for what seemed like forever to get a drink.

"So, Krista, what do you do for fun?" Troy stood closer to her and spoke into her ear.

Her cheeks turned pink once again. I had a feeling she liked him from their first glance, because Krista usually wasn't shy around boys she wasn't interested in. I couldn't help but give myself a pat on the back for that match made.

"Not much, really. I hang out with this nut over here a lot. That's about it." She poked me with her finger, and we all laughed.

The music was booming to a fun beat, sending vibrations throughout my body, and I really wanted to dance. Krista and Troy were engaged in conversation. I decided to give them some privacy, so I got up to walk around and look at the scenery.

A guy standing at the bar caught my eye, and I found I couldn't look away. I wasn't sure any woman could. He was gorgeous, tall and muscular with thick chestnut hair that gave me the urge to run my twitching fingers through it. The tan button-down he wore over the tight white T-shirt didn't cover up enough of his muscles. My fingers itched to touch his chest and, seriously, I could have kissed whoever made those jeans. I would have followed him anywhere just for the view.

He turned and caught me staring, and I quickly averted my eyes to the picture over the bar. It was the ugliest piece of art I'd ever seen, but I hoped he would think I'd been admiring it—or trying to figure out if it was a guitar or a badly broken violin—rather than staring at his better assets in those jeans.

Oh, my goodness! Was he walking toward me? He was. He had pushed away from the bar and was headed in my direction.

"Okay, stay cool, Jai," I whispered, trying to remember how to breathe. "You got this, girl. Just relax."

As he got closer, I felt the butterflies in my stomach flutter around. Please don't throw up, Jai.

"Hello, beautiful, would you like to dance?" He held his hand out to me.

I just stood there like a rag doll, my mind a complete blank. All I could do was stare into his eyes. They were a sparkling blue that had me hypnotized by their beauty. I was certain they were laughing at me, causing me to snap out of my hormone-induced trance I had fallen into.

"Um, sure," I finally managed to blurt out, then stumbled forward as I tripped over my own foot. "I'm not a great dancer, but if you're willing to take the risk, I'm game."

"Well, you're in luck." He grabbed my hand to lead me out on the dance floor. "My name is Corbin Alexander, and I'm an excellent teacher."

Once we were on the floor, he pulled my arms up around his neck and wrapped his around my waist. I rested my face against his chest to hide my rosy cheeks. He smelled wonderful, like sandalwood and coriander. When I finally got up the courage to look up at him again, he was smiling.

"See, I told you I'm a good teacher," he whispered.

I just smiled back at him. He really was good. Too good, in fact. The music picked up, and we decided to find a table to talk.

"Where are you from?" he asked once we were settled in a booth in the darkest corner of the club.

"Well, I grew up in and out of foster homes, so I'm kind of from all over. How about you?"

"I grew up in a small town not too far from here called Asher Grove." He placed his drink on a cork coaster. "I tend to travel a lot for work, but I enjoy being home as often as I can. Was it tough growing up in the system?"

"Well, I don't know about tough, but I'm glad to finally be on my own, that's for sure." I took a sip of my tea.

Krista and Troy walked up, and I started to introduce them to Corbin when I realized I hadn't even given him my name yet.

I cleared my throat. "I'm Jai, and these two are my friends, Krista and Troy. This is Corbin Alexander."

Krista gave me a thumbs up that only I could see, and I had to fight hard not to laugh.

"It's loud in here," Troy said. "Why don't we all go out for coffee where we can actually hear one another talk?"

We all agreed and headed across the street to the Vanilla Bean, a small twenty-four-hour coffee shop that had the most amazing iced coffee.

"I love the smell of this place," Krista said. She made a loud sniffing sound as we entered the café. The shop was filled with the rich scent of ground coffee and fresh baked muffins. My stomach growled in response to the wonderful smell.

"What kind of music are you guys in the mood for?" Troy asked.

"Well," I said, "I prefer Enya with my coffee, if that's okay with everyone here."

Everyone agreed it was fine. Troy walked over to the juke box in the far corner of the room and dropped two quarters into the machine and selected the chosen album. We were the only customers in the shop, so we sat at the table closest to the juke box, and it didn't take long for us to receive service.

"What can I get you?" The short blonde waitress asked. Her nametag revealed the name Jan, although she didn't introduce herself. I ordered a blueberry muffin and a caramel cappuccino. Everyone else gave her their orders, and she walked away.

The silence unnerved me. Krista claims I have a lack of "man skills" and I was determined to prove her wrong, so I blurted out the first thing that came to me. "So, what do you do for a living, Corbin?"

"I'm a bodyguard of sorts," he answered.

"Oh, that sounds dangerous." Krista kicked me in the shin under the table.

I rolled my eyes in response. The waitress delivered our orders to the table and I took a big drink of my cappuccino.

"I'll be your bodyguard, if you let me," he said to me and bounced his eyebrows up and down suggestively, causing me to laugh and choke on my coffee.

"Oh, you will, will you? Because I'm a lot to handle." We all busted out laughing.

We had a wonderful time just talking about random stuff. I never thought I could feel this happy and perfectly normal at the same time.

"Well, speaking of bodyguards, it's getting late and the big bad wolf might be out there waiting for us," Krista said—overdramatically, with a pouty lip. "Would you strong young men like to walk the two of us home?"

"Sure," they both said simultaneously.

Corbin paid our bill even though we all told him not to. He was kind and mannerly, and I was secretly proud he was with me.

The crisp wind was fierce outside, and it made me shiver. Corbin put his arm around me to warm me up. It was nice, being close to him, but weird at the same time since I didn't typically want to be close to anyone.

I'd never been one to warm up to people quickly, but there was something about him that made me feel safe.

There were clouds in the sky, hiding the stars from our view, but I didn't require their beauty. I had Corbin to look at.

"I hear the fair is in town this weekend. Would you guys all like to meet up there tomorrow night at six o'clock," Corbin asked?

We all agreed. It sounded like fun, and I was glad to have another outing to look forward to.

Too soon, we arrived outside my apartment. I hated for the night to end. I was having such a wonderful time with Krista and my new friends. Corbin picked up my hand and placed a soft kiss on it instead of saying goodbye. Troy gave Krista an intimate hug. Then the guys left, and Krista and I went inside.

"That was quite a hug you got there," I teased as we walked up the steps.

"It was just a hug," she said, but a huge smile formed on her face. I knew it was more than just a hug. I also knew Krista would probably talk my ear off all night about how dreamy Troy was.

We opened the door and got settled in for the night. While Krista was in the shower, I lay in bed reflecting on the night. My memory was focused on every detail, from Corbin's chest to his chiseled jaw line. My body tingled in response to my thoughts.

"Corbin Alexander." His name rolled off my tongue like a pat of honey butter. I must have fallen asleep before Krista came out, because the next thing I remember, I woke to my regularly scheduled nightmare.

***

We met up at the fairgrounds promptly at six. The sun was setting, allowing us enough light to navigate through the crowd before it got dark. We got our armbands and then discussed what to ride first. We ended up riding everything, from the Tilt-A-Whirl to the Graviton.

"Do you want to go ride the Ferris wheel?" Corbin asked.

"I would love to," I replied. Since Krista wasn't a fan of the Ferris wheel, she and Troy headed to the cotton candy stand, instead.

The full moon was a big beautiful circle of white light in the now dark sky. Colored lights surrounded us in every direction, allowing us to see our surroundings a little more clearly.

The ride was amazing, and Corbin grabbed my hand several times and held it tight. I wasn't sure how to react, so I just enjoyed the affection.

"That was so much fun," I said as we exited the gate at the ride.

"It was a lot of fun," Corbin said, still holding my hand. "I'm glad we got to come out here tonight."

"Thank you for inviting us." Then it dawned on me that I was getting attached to him, and in such a short amount of time. I wasn't sure if I should be excited or scared.

We went looking for Krista and Troy. Between the busy crowd and the dark night sky, it was difficult to distinguish who was who. I went into the ladies' bathroom to see if perhaps she had gone in there.

"Hello," I called out as I looked underneath stall doors for feet. It was empty. I walked out, and someone grabbed me from behind. His massive hand held my mouth closed and pushed the back of my head firmly against his chest. His breath smelled of rotten flesh, and vomit rose in my throat.

"If you want to keep your friend safe, you better find that amulet, little wolf," he snarled and released me from his grip. My heart pounded so hard, I felt it in my ears. I turned around, but he'd disappeared, leaving Krista's scarf on the ground.

I was frantic, and I ran as fast as I could through the crowd, screaming out my friends' names at the top of my lungs. I was so scared that I didn't even see the three of them coming toward me until I ran right into them.

"Jai, honey, what's wrong?" Krista pulled me close to her.

"You're okay?" I sobbed as I looked up at her.

"Of course, I'm okay." She gave me a questioning look.

"Some foul-smelling creep jumped me outside the bathroom, threatening to hurt you if I didn't bring him some stupid amulet." I wiped my eyes with the back of my hand. "He left your scarf, and I thought he had you. I was so scared, and I didn't know how to help you because I don't have any idea what he's talking about."

"So that's where it went!" Krista took the scarf from me. "I thought I lost it on one of the rides earlier."

Corbin pulled me and Krista close to him and inspected our surroundings. I was still shaking from that evil man's touch. Krista held onto me tightly, and Troy surveyed the crowd in front of us for anyone suspicious.

"What did this guy look like?" Corbin asked while still scanning the area.

"I don't know, he disappeared into the darkness. The scarf is the only evidence I have of him."

"I think we should call it a night just in case this guy is still out there." Corbin took my hand and pulled me toward the entrance. "How are you girls getting home?"

"We rode the bus, but in light of the situation, I'm not sure that's a clever idea," Krista said. "Troy, do you have your taxi here?"

"No, I had a friend drop me off," Troy replied. "My taxi isn't far from your apartment, if you want me to ride the bus home with you. I can walk to my car once you girls are home."

"I'll take you guys back to Jai's apartment," Corbin said as he practically dragged me along with his brisk gait. "I would feel better knowing everyone got home safely, anyway."

We all piled into his yellow mustang. I still felt shaky and couldn't get the foul smell of that monster's breath out nose. I felt dirty being near that creep. All I could think about was a hot shower.

Corbin drove fast but safely on our route home, and I was thankful for the short trip. He opened the door for me, and I climbed out if his car. We all walked up the steps quietly and before we got to the main entrance, he stopped and pushed me behind him.

"Wait. Something's wrong." Corbin looked around the building. "Troy, stay here with the girls while I run upstairs and make sure everything is clear."

We waited for a few minutes before I got restless and followed him. My apartment had been ransacked. My stuff was everywhere. Even my mattress had been sliced. Feathers still fell from the ceiling. We must have just missed... whomever had done this. My eyes filled with hot tears.

"Why?" I whispered, trying to hold in my disappointment. "What would anyone want with my things? I don't have anything of value. I don't even own a computer."

"Well, someone thought you had something, and they wanted it pretty badly," Corbin said, with his jaw tight. "We need to call the police. Do you girls have a place to stay tonight?"

"Yeah, we can stay at my place," Krista volunteered. "It's only three blocks from here. It's within walking distance"

"I would like to stay and look around a little, after the officers get here, to see if I can find anything out about who may have done this," Corbin said while he dialed the number to the station. "I have a friend at the police station who can come do a report. If that's okay with you Jai?"

"Yeah, that's okay. I'm just ready to get out of here." My grief had turned to anger as I looked at my things scattered around.

"Troy, do you think you could drive us to Krista's house after the police report?"

The officer arrived quickly, and the report didn't take long to file. He looked around and wrote some notes on his report and asked a few very basic questions before he had me sign the report and instructed me to keep my doors locked. He and Corbin talked quietly while I attempted to gather some of my toiletries and clothes for the night.

"I'm ready if you guys are." I said. I walked over to where Troy was standing.

"Yeah, girls, let's get out of here!" Troy replied as he grabbed Krista's hand. I gave Corbin a quick hug and a peck on the cheek.

"Thank you," I said. He grabbed a notepad and jotted down his phone number and slipped it into the back pocket of my skirt, then he kissed my hand.

"If it's the last thing I do, I will figure out who did this, and I will make them pay dearly for hurting you, Jai. I promise you that much." Corbin stared into my tear-filled eyes.

I know I'd only just met him, but I believed with all my heart that he was telling me the truth. I could feel it.

I really didn't want to leave without him, but I guessed, as a bodyguard, he had at least some experience with this kind of thing. In the end, Krista, Troy, and I headed for his cab, leaving Corbin behind to look around the apartment.

"Where is your taxi?" I scanned the empty parking lot for Troy's car.

"It's at Rauling Park." he pointed over his right shoulder.

"Krista's house is about three blocks away from here, and your taxi is only a block away if we cut through the park." I pointed in the general directions. "It will be faster this way." We started on our journey down the half-lit street.

The park was dark, and that made me nervous, but we all knew it was faster than walking all the way through town. Krista suggested using the alley between my apartment building and the park, since it would come out almost exactly where Troy said the cab was parked. I would have preferred not to, but I really didn't feel comfortable on the street, either. Finally, I agreed that it was the best plan, and we headed down the alley.

There was something oddly familiar about the alley. I jumped as the wind caused the lid of the empty dumpster at the end of the alley to bang loudly. The sound made my hair stand on end as goosebumps filled my arms. That sound echoed another metallic banging I was all too familiar with. When my heart started to race and sweat started popping out on my forehead, I knew we'd made a terrible mistake.

"Wait, we have to go back. We have to go back to the street!" I cried frantically, grabbed Krista's hand, and pulled her toward the street as I realized I was in the alley from my nightmares.

Troy just kept walking faster, pulling harder on Krista's other arm.

"Troy!" I screamed in full panic mode. "We have to go back!"

He turned around, and his eyes were glowing bright crimson. Krista screamed as she fought to free her hand from his grip. He was the monster hiding in the shadows all along. This man I thought to be so kind was something completely different. I was in shock and couldn't move.

"Oh, sweet wolf. You and your pretty little friend are not going anywhere," he growled while wrapping his hand around Krista's neck and licking her cheek. "You have something of mine, and now I have something of yours. Until I get the amulet your thieving parents took from me, I'm keeping her."

"What are you? What are you talking about?" I cried out loudly. "I don't know what you're talking about. I don't have anything. I don't even know who my parents are! Now let us go, please."

I was getting angry, and something built up inside me.

"That's right, get angry, little wolf," he said and began to laugh. "See yourself for what you really are—a monster!"

His words stunned me. What if I was the monster?

Either way, he wasn't going to hurt the only person in the entire world I cared about. The next thing I saw was a blast of light. I threw my hand up and managed to block the flames before they engulfed me, causing me to fall backward and land on the ground—hard. While I was distracted by the flames, he disappeared, taking Krista with him.

"No!" I screamed. I ran after them but was too late. They were already gone. And as the thought that I might never see my best friend again crossed my mind, I fell to my knees and sobbed. Not only had I lost my best friend I had been betrayed by another, and it hurt like hell.

Chapter Four

THE COMPOUND

"Jai, Jai, is that you, where are you?" I heard Corbin yelling from a distance. My heartbeat still pounded in my ears. My eyes were swollen, which made it hard to see, but I knew I needed him, so I clumsily stood up and ran out of the alley until I bumped into him. Still sobbing, I tried to explain what happened.

"It was—" I hiccupped from my excessive crying. "It was Troy. He took her, there is something seriously wrong with him."

He reached down under my arms to comfort me with a tight embrace.

"Let's get you out of here." He picked me up and carried me back to my apartment. I was fully capable of walking, but his scent was calming. I buried my face into his chest to hide from my surroundings in fear of what was out there watching me. He went up the stairs with ease, as if I didn't weigh more than a feather.

We entered the apartment, and he locked the door. He gently set me down on the couch and brought me some Kleenex, then he sat down beside me.

"Jai, what did he say to you?" Corbin lifted my chin with his index finger.

I dried my tears with the tissue he gave me. "He said my parents took something of his and he wants it back, but I don't have anything." I wiped my excessively running nose. "The only thing I have of my parents is a stupid box of riddles and old useless maps." I threw my arm up in the air.

"Jai, can I see this box?" he asked.

"Oh, my gosh! What if they got it?" I jumped up, ran over to the bed, climbed up, and reached for the ceiling. When I removed the tile, I let out a sigh of relief. "It's still here."

I pulled the box down. "I'm not sure how to open it, the first time it just opened up on its own."

"Jai, who were your parents?" He looked worried.

"Roberta and Jimmy Weaver, according to the letter inside of this blasted sealed box." I handed it over to him.

"This box has been spelled with some pretty strong magic and will only open if you want it to open." He inspected the detail on the box then handed it back to me. "It will not open for anyone other than you."

"How do you know about this stuff?" I blew my nose in my Kleenex again.

"Well, I told you I was a bodyguard, which is true, I am. I'm just a bodyguard of many people. And so are you. It's why you feel so safe around me," he explained as he began to pace around while he talked. "We are known as The Protectors. Although we all have different gifts, we have a common goal. To protect the innocent, no matter the cost.

"What I don't understand is what happened to your parents. They have been missing for eighteen years. Everyone in the compound thought they were dead, but the elders have always said they were very much alive." He scratched his head, trying to make sense of the situation.

"If they are not with you and you don't know who and what you are, then where are they?" He rubbed his hand through his hair and concentrated on the box in my hands.

"Look, Corbin, I don't know anything about anything right now. I just want to get my friend back from that red-eyed, arrogant monster. If I'm some bad-ass bodyguard, I sure am lacking all the essential skills for the job."

"We need to get you to the compound, where you'll be safe. It'll allow us to figure out who and what is after you, and what exactly they think you have of theirs." He paced my messy living room. "We need to leave as soon as possible." He grabbed a plastic bag and threw some of my clothes in it.

"Wait, how do I know I can trust you?" I said, with a cold look on my face. I mean the last guy I trusted turned into a hot-headed demon kidnapper. "Why should I just pick up and run away with you?"

"Look Jai, I know you don't know me, but I assure you I only want to help you." He walked toward me and grabbed my hand. "I promise you that I will help you figure all of this out." He let go of my hand and placed the bag in its place.

"Fine, but if you go all red eyed on me I will not hesitate to snap your neck. I was raised to defend myself." I said with a firm tone and turned away from him. I wasn't in the mood to talk anymore, so I stood up and helped gather my essential items. Then we left my apartment.

He held my hand as we walked to his car. When we got there, he opened the door for me. I climbed inside and buckled my seatbelt. I still felt the physical effects of my uncontrolled crying which caused my eyes to be heavy. And I was mentally exhausted.

"It's about an hour away. You should try to rest, if you can." He handed me a small black cover, then he turned the key and the mustang purred to life.

I dozed off. I woke several times only to see those red eyes drilling into my subconscious, making my stomach knot up. I knew I needed to call Momma Jane and tell her about Krista, but I couldn't bring myself to make the call. I figured I'd land myself in a little straight jacket if I told them she was abducted by a red-eyed demon. I decided I would call her and leave out those details.

I dialed the number with nervous fingers. I didn't know what to say to her, so I decided I would have to lie. Guilt filled me when she answered the line.

"Jai, honey, thank goodness you called! I have been so worried." Her voice sounded muffled like maybe she had been crying. "Is Krista there? I need to talk to her." I understood her urgency and I hated myself for not calling her sooner.

"She is ok, but she isn't here right now. We decided to take a last-minute girls trip to the beach for a few days." I tried to sound upbeat. "Krista forgot her phone in my apartment, so you should be able to reach us on mine when we are not at the beach."

"Well, when Krista gets back please have her call me? I have been worried sick. Are you sure you two are okay?"

"Yes, we are fine. We will call you again soon." We hung up the phone and I dried the tears that had escaped my eyes.

***

"We're here." Corbin said cheerfully, causing me to sit up in my seat. There was a massive brick wall, but no gate to enter. We got out of the car and walked toward the wall.

"How do we get inside?" I walked closer and put my hand on the solid brick.

"Want to see something really cool?" He grabbed my free hand and pulled me closer to him, causing me to trip over my foot in the process. He put his hand on the wall and mumbled, "Bubbles." The wall disappeared into thin air, leaving nothing but open space.

"How did you do that?" I looked around to see if I was on Candid Camera or some crazy reality TV show. Relieved no one was lurking with a video camera, I walked through the empty space.

"I told you, there is magic within us, and we'll find yours." He smiled down at me. We climbed back in the car, and I looked out the back window as we drove off to see the wall reappear, making me feel like I was stuck in a dream.

"Your magic word is 'bubbles', seriously?" I laughed as I slid back into my seat and looked out the window to see we were surrounded by trees as we drove down the little dirt road.

"Well, there was this cartoon when I was little, and it's been that ever since." He shrugged his shoulders and grinned at me with his ravishing smile, causing my cheeks to burn.

"Well, it does beat boring 'abracadabra'." I laughed with relief. I had seen magic at work, and there was someone who would be able to help me figure it out.

"Welcome to the Compound," Corbin said cheerfully as we passed a sign to our right that read 'Asher Grove'. The gravel road looked long and was surrounded by more beautiful trees. Their leaves were scattered around the ground, leaving shades of mustard, orange, and brown in the soft light of the crescent moon.

"I think you will be safer staying here for a while. Besides, I have plenty of room at my place, and you will eventually move into your parents' home. Once it's been cleaned up a bit, that is. It's been empty since they disappeared." He winked at me. "But for now, it looks like you're stuck with me." A big cheesy smile crossed his face.

"Well, I guess it beats staying with my monster friend, Troy." I stared out the window. "I'm just ready to find Krista. That's all I'm worried about right now."

"Don't worry, love. We'll find her, but first we have to figure out how." He placed his hand on my thigh and squeezed.

I squirmed away. It felt nice, but it terrified me, all the same.

"Tonight, we'll head over to my place and get settled in. Tomorrow, I'll give you a tour of the compound and introduce you to the Elders." A yawned escaped his mouth.

We turned down a bricked road and in front of us sprawled a very large white plantation style house with a big magnolia tree in the front. It was breathtaking, and I couldn't stop staring at it.

"That, sweet Jai, is the Weaver home. Which means, it's your home once the Elders verify your bloodline." He pointed at the house.

"Wait! What? That beautiful house is mine?" I squealed and flipped up to stare out the back window as we drove past the house. "This all feels like a crazy dream."

"This is the Alexander house. My house, to be exact." Corbin gave me a proud look. "My parents have their house at the back of the lot, and I had this one built a few years ago. It's one of the newer houses in the compound." He turned the car engine off and opened the door.

We got out of the car, and I stood in awe, gaping at his home. It wasn't as big as the Weaver house, but it didn't lack beauty. It was a log cabin type house, but larger, with a lovely wraparound porch decorated with colored lights and wicker rocking chairs. Tall trees marked his property line.

I breathed in the sweet smell of the cool night air just before Corbin opened the door and welcomed me inside.

"Your home is very charming." I smiled up at him.

"Thank you. I'll give you the grand tour tomorrow, but let's rest now." He put his hand on my lower back and led me down a hallway.

My skin tingled as his hand touched my back. We bypassed the living room and kitchen.

"This room to the right is my room, if you need me. Your room is across the hall." He opened my door and flipped on the light, revealing the gorgeous room.

It was lilac purple and trimmed in cream. The canopy bed was full of fluffy pillows and looked like it should belong to a princess. There was a tall maple armoire just across from the door. I let out a gasp and walked inside.

"Well, if you like this part, just wait until you see the bathroom." Corbin smiled from ear to ear.

I walked to the bathroom and stood in absolute amazement. A big Jacuzzi tub stood just in front of a walk-through shower.

The room smelled of fresh roses and was decorated to match the bedroom. The mirror lined the wall above the sink and was lit up by six candle-shaped light fixtures. There was a makeup counter, fully stocked with fancy makeup, and a small stool was placed under the counter. Why did he have all this girl stuff in his house?

"Corbin, thank you for letting me stay here, and thank you for being so kind." I looked up at him, hoping these wasn't his girlfriend's things. I had never seen such kindness, and we had only known each other a short while. I was confused as to how I should act in return.

He picked up my hand, and tiny electric shivers ran up my arm in response to his touch. I didn't understand why he had such an effect on me. He lifted my hand to his soft lips and planted a gentle kiss on it. I almost melted on the spot.

"It is my pleasure, beautiful," he said in a silky voice. Then he turned to walk out of the room, but stopped just before he got to the door.

"There are some clothes in the closet that should fit you, and plenty of girlie stuff in that bathroom. Help yourself to whatever you need. My sister, Mandi, stays here when she visits, and she leaves a supply of everything she owns because she's too lazy to pack. So, she probably has you covered. Tomorrow, we can get anything you need that isn't here. In the meantime, I'm off to bed. If you need me, please don't be afraid to wake me." And he closed the door.

I didn't know what I wanted to do first— try out that bathtub or jump on that fluffy bed. A yawn escaped my mouth, which told me my body had made the decision for me.

I opened the closet to find several pastel nightgowns and some fresh underwear on the shelf. It was hard to choose which one to wear because they were all beautiful. I picked one out and changed. I hardly recognized myself when I looked in the mirror.

I was breathtaking. The pale green satin gown complimented my still swollen jade eyes while the low-cut lace in the front showed just enough skin to be sexy.

I walked over to the bed, removed about ten perfectly placed pillows, and put them on the love seat. Then I climbed into the comfortable bed and was asleep in minutes.

I woke to a soft knock at the door. Yawning, I got up and made my way over and opened it, realizing it was morning and for the first time I could remember, I didn't have my nightmare.

Of course, I had lived it the night before.

"Good morning, sunshine," Corbin said and handed me a cup of coffee. He quickly averted his gaze, and I realized I was still in my nightgown. His reaction lead me to believe he liked what he saw, and I was secretly pleased.

"Thanks, and good morning." I set my coffee down on the dresser and grabbed a robe.

"Walter and Mary will be over shortly to meet you and to verify your DNA." He stared at his feet. "Then, we can begin our tour of the compound and get a training schedule together. I made you breakfast." He seemed excited for me to eat what he cooked.

"You cooked for me?" I asked.

"Well, yes, I'm not going to let you starve. I didn't know what you like, so I made a lot of stuff. Hope you're hungry." He chuckled.

I walked into the kitchen to find pancakes, waffles, omelets, and fresh fruit.

The kitchen was amazing. It was tiled in gunmetal gray and had a center island with a small vegetable sink in it. There was a stainless steel double oven and a massive gas stove. I figured he enjoyed cooking from the layout of the kitchen and the wonderful breakfast spread out for me.

"You did all of this for me?" I piled a plate full of food. No one had ever cooked like that for me. I was used to fending for myself. Even when I was little, it was cereal and frozen burritos out of the microwave. "Corbin, you're a man of many trades." I swallowed a big bite of my omelet. "This is delicious, thank you." And I continued to stuff my mouth.

"You, my dear, are very welcome, and I am honored you like it." He took a bow. We both laughed.

"Who are Mary and Walter, and is this DNA thing going to hurt?" I asked, feeling nervous.

"They are two of the Elders, and no, it will not hurt. I promise." He looked straight into my eyes. It felt like he could see right through to my soul, and I enjoyed every second of it.

We finished up breakfast and cleaned the kitchen together. We worked perfectly in sync with one another. I washed and rinsed while he dried and put away.

I would steal a glance at him from time to time when he wasn't looking. He was so handsome, even in his plain white T-shirt and jogging pants. He had a tattoo around his left arm in the form of a tribal band, and his sleeve barely covered it due to his muscles. Not too big, and not too small.

He was perfectly built, and I wondered how I'd managed to meet him again. I was lost deep in thought when Corbin managed to snap me out of it. "They're here." He sounded almost too chipper.

Why was he so excited about helping me, anyway? Maybe to help solve the puzzle of the missing Weaver couple, AKA my parents.

Well, either way, I was grateful for his hospitality and protection.

Corbin grabbed my hand as we walked to the front door to meet Walter and Mary. They were older than I expected. Mary was lovely, her white hair curled in tight spirals around her round face. Her baby blue eyes twinkled as she smiled and reached out to shake my hand. She was short and plump and reminded me of an old Santa picture with Mrs. Claus. Walter was tall and slender; his dark hair was streaked with gray throughout. He was very tan and dressed in a flannel shirt and a pair of blue jean coveralls. I assumed him to be an outdoorsy, gardening-type man.

Like Mary, he also had baby blue eyes, and I immediately felt safe and, odd as it seemed, I felt loved by them. Walter gave me a big hug instead of shaking my hand and at that moment, I knew I loved them, too.

"Where would you like to set up?" Corbin asked after he welcomed them inside.

"How about the garden out back?" Walter pointed to the French doors leading to the backyard.

Mary just smiled, shook her head, and whispered, "That man loves the great outdoors." I got the impression they were married, although Corbin didn't mention that to me.

We walked out to the garden area. What a lovely place. Perfectly maintained flower beds despite the cooler temperatures, and beautiful statues of women and children decorated the landscape.

There was a wooden bench over by a birdbath that looked inviting to me. It would make a perfect reading spot. I giggled as I passed a small area where spinach, collard greens, and kale grew in abundance. I didn't picture Corbin as a greens-and-beans kind of guy.

Even though the scenery seemed to take the edge off my nerves, I was still worried. I understood we were preparing to verify my DNA. It was supposed to be a good thing, but what if it wasn't?

What if I wasn't Jaime Grace Weaver? What if Sister Ann Marie gave me someone else's key? Ready or not, it was time to find out.

Chapter Five

UNBOUND

"So, Walter and Mary will perform an incantation in attempt to unbind you," Corbin explained as we walked over to a cement bench and sat down. "In the process, it should reveal your DNA via colors of your aura."

Mary placed a small wooden chair directly in front of the bench. I felt the warm sun settle on my face, and I welcomed its relaxing gleam. It was time to reveal my true colors, literally.

"Jai, love, I need you to sit on this chair and close your eyes," Mary said with a low and caring voice as she patted the chair in front of me. "Walter, Corbin, and I will be chanting as we hold hands around you. Do not attempt to chant with us, do not stand up, and last but of most importance, do not open your eyes."

"Yes, ma'am." My voice cracked a little. My body was tensed and nervous. I focused my attention on the sun's inviting rays as they connected their hands together.

"It's time to close your eyes, dear. This won't take long, and I'll tell you when you can open them," Walter said.

I did as I was told and focused on the sun's warmth again.

"Picture a belt around Jai's waist. You must believe it's there. Imagine it beaming bright silver as the magic is released from the belt and into her body," Mary instructed, to Walter and Corbin, in a low soothing tone of voice. "Focus like your life depends on it. Envision the belt lose power and turn black as Jai gets stronger. Now, repeat after me." In a louder, more serious voice, she said, "With the power of three, we unbind thee."

They repeated it, over and over, for what seemed like forever.

I grew impatient.

I was not sure what was supposed to happen, but I didn't feel any different. They got quiet for a moment, and I wanted to open my eyes, but I restrained myself from doing so.

"Mary, what color is the belt?" Walter asked.

"It's black, completely black," she replied.

"Corbin, is the buckle fastened?" Walter whispered.

"Yes, sir, it is still fastened."

"It appears it will take more time to regain her full power, but we have managed to release a good deal. Her parents enforced the spell in stages, and it will just take time for her full potential to emerge," Walter explained. "They must have been afraid for her life."

"They were hiding her from something or someone, and this was to ensure that in the event she was captured, only a fraction of her power would show." Mary paced blindly around me. "Thus, they would never know her full potential. She is very powerful and in the wrong hands could bring mass destruction."

"We will begin teaching her to use what has been restored tomorrow morning. You can open your eyes now," Walter said.

I was beginning to think it wasn't working until that moment. Everyone stared at me with open mouths. Could we say "Awkward!"?

I opened my mouth to ask what was so interesting when I realized I was floating. In the air. Oh, sweet mother of trolls, I was floating!

"Guys, a little help here would be nice." I squealed and squirmed in the chair, afraid I would slip off and fall.

"Somebody... Anybody, want to tell me how to get down from here?" I screamed, as I was getting annoyed.

"Sunshine, calm down and picture yourself slowly lowering to the ground," Mary calmly said as she put her hands in front of her and lowered them to the ground.

"Okay, here goes." I pictured myself slowly lowering to the ground over and over, rather quickly, as my heart pounded, and my entire body trembled in fear. I hit the ground rather abruptly with a thud, causing the chair to splinter beneath me. I should have kept my eyes open. I quickly realized I would be feeling that fall later.

"Well, that could have been much worse." I stood up and smiled at the group. They were all looking past me like I was invisible. I turned around to see what they were looking at, and I saw the most beautiful pink and gold swirling light in front of me. It was so bright, I could barely see beyond it. Wait... there was someone in the light. A woman, a beautiful woman.

"Jai, my sweet baby girl. I have waited for so long to see you. I cannot stay for long, as I am being held prisoner, and they can sense when I attempt to reach out. You hold the key to finding us inside yourself.

"Don't be afraid to be what you are destined to be. There is a room in our family home. Your bracelet is the key to unlocking the door and finding the answers you seek.

"Please hurry, my child. I fear your father and I cannot last much longer. Your

grandparents and Corbin will keep you safe."
She pointed to Walter and Mary.

"Mom, Dad, it's so good to see you. I miss you both so much. I love you, but I must go now before they know what I am doing. Please keep her safe." Then she faded away.

We all just stood there for a minute, looking at each other. A tear rolled down Mary's cheek. It just seemed natural to go to her, so I walked over and hugged her. I no longer felt awkward with physical gestures.

I suppose that was what I was missing all my life—how natural it felt to care for someone. Even though we had only just met, at that moment, my entire heart went out to her.

"I will find them. I don't know how yet, but I give you my word. I will bring my parents back," I said, while still embraced in Mary's arms. Walter walked up to me and took my hand. I looked up at him to see he, too, was crying.

"We found you. We have been looking for you for so long, and now you are here." He wrapped his arms around Mary and me. "My dear grandchild, how I have waited for the day I would hold you in my arms." We sat there embraced for a good bit before Corbin spoke.

"I hate to interrupt, but this demonic creature has Krista hostage, as well. We need to figure out where and what exactly he is as soon as possible."

I released my grandparents. "Wait, you mean there is more than one kind of demon?"

"There are several types of demons, angry spirits, and yes, even the devil," Corbin said. "They range from annoying and harmless to deadly, and they all have one thing in common—they want to cause havoc and get revenge on innocent souls."

"We have found a ghost or two that has come back to help or check on us from time to time," Mary said. "So, not all are evil, but the majority are."

"How do we find out what Troy really is?" I asked.

"Well, for a start, we get your home cleaned up and ready for you." Corbin walked over and put his arm around my shoulders. "While we are doing that, you need to be trained. We need to find out what abilities you have. I have a feeling it's going to take all of us to get your parents and Krista back."

"These things must maintain a lot of energy to trap and hold your parents." Walter picked up the pieces of the broken chair. "They were the strongest in the compound."

"Jai, this is going to be a rocky road, but from the looks of it, you are just as strong or even stronger than your parents." Mary brought out a garbage can to collect the wooden pieces from Walter. "With the entire compound behind you, we will get them back."

"You can stay with me until your home is ready, if you want," Corbin said.

Mary winked at Walter, and I had to fight to hold in my grin and hide my embarrassment. "That would be great, thank you."

"I think it's time we have a council meeting," Walter said as we walked back inside the house. "I'll let you know how it goes later." We hugged again, and I walked my grandparents to the door.

"I am so thankful to have found you, dear." Mary hugged me tight. "From now on you should call us Grams and Gramps, if you want." Mary said and winked at me.

I smiled back at them. Their eyes sparkled with happiness and it made me feel good. "Thank you, Grams, I will see you both later." I smiled and closed the door behind them, and watched through the window as they walked away hand in hand.

"Well, that was interesting, but other than being emotionally wiped out, I don't feel any different." I held up my arms to show my nonexistent muscles and laughed. "Shouldn't I be feeling all powerful and stuff?"

"Not really. I mean, the power was always there, just dormant inside you." Corbin handed me a glass of water. "You will feel it once you start accessing it. We can start training after we tour the compound, if you want."

"How will I know what I can do and what I can't do?" I brushed off the bottom of my shirt to remove some of the dirt from my fall.

"There are different tests you can do, but most of the time you just learn as you go."

"What are your abilities or powers?" I asked as I gulped down the icy water.

"Speed for one. I am insanely fast. I can't teleport, but I'm a close second. Strength, I may not look like it, but if I wanted to, I could throw an eighteen-wheeler over my entire house. Last, but not least, I can control fire. Which means I can start it, throw it, catch it, and snuff it out. Pretty impressive, huh?" He waggled his eyebrows at me.

"What if I don't even have any powers? Or what if I do, but they are nothing compared to my parents'? If they couldn't stop this thing together, how am I supposed to do it by myself?"

"First of all, you will not be by yourself. I will be right beside you, and so will the other scouts in the compound. Second, there is no way you have no powers. How do you think I found you? How do you think Troy found you? It's your essence," he explained as he sat down beside me at the kitchen table. "Your magical essence lets off a slight vibration, and the stronger you get, the stronger the vibration will be.

"The bind started losing power either because you are getting older and stronger, or because your parents are getting weaker and so is their magic. I couldn't tell how strong you were, and I had no idea who you were, but I knew without a doubt you were one of us."

"Us? What are we, exactly?" I was unsure about my new-found destiny, so the more information, the better. "Is that why you decided to talk to me? Because of my magical essence?" I tried to hide the disappointment in my voice, but it was hard.

"No, I decided to talk to you because I wanted to talk to you." He walked over and picked up my magical box. "I didn't even feel your essence until we were on the dance floor. It isn't very strong, but apparently strong enough that Troy felt it at some point as well." He handed me the box. "I know this is a lot of information, but if you want to save Krista then you need to trust me."

"I'll go with you, but I can't promise that I will trust anyone ever again." I wasn't sure what I believed at that point. I knew two things for certain—I had to learn to fight, and life as I once knew it was gone forever, which terrified me even more.

Chapter Six

WHAT AM I?

"Jai, we are known as The Protectors." Corbin placed a bowl of fruit on the table in front of us. "We are born with special abilities—powers, as some call them—to protect the innocent from anything evil.

We all have different talents and come from different families. Most of us live here at the compound, but some choose to live elsewhere. Occasionally, we meet a drifter that doesn't know what he or she is due to a one-night stand kind of situation, but other than that, we keep to ourselves." He began to peel an orange.

"Some of us call ourselves scouts or hunters, but the technical term written in our history manuals is 'protectors'. We have certain rules set forth by the elders. Sometimes, we break a rule and there are different consequences for each rule broken. Like practicing for self-gain or using our power to harm innocents." He ate one of the freshly peeled orange segments.

"You'll get all the details soon. It's not all bad. We mostly get to hang out and practice all day. We hunt once a week, which means we go out making sure everything is okay." He popped another piece of the juicy orange into his mouth.

"Sometimes we're sent far away, other times an hour or less. Just depends on where there has been suspicious activity."

"You said the Elders would confirm my DNA. Does that mean my grandparents are Elders?" I asked, just to clarify that I was following everything correctly.

"Yes, they are. As you will be one day when they pass on. See, the Elders are direct ancestors of the founding fathers. They are made up of the five original families who built this compound, The Weavers, The Alexanders, The Nolan's, The Whitlows and the Tabell's." He cleaned up his orange peel and threw it in the trash.

"The Whitlow's and the Tabell's lines ended when their offspring were unable to reproduce. So, now it's just the three remaining families. Your ancestors are the Weavers and the Nolan's, two founding families, as your father is a Weaver and your mother a Nolan. Your father was on the council when he disappeared. So, technically, that is your place to fill should you choose to do so.

There are lots of other families in the compound, and there has been talk of anointing two more families. It's only just been put up to vote, though, so I'm not sure what will come of that. Enough politics." He threw a pair of white tennis shoes at me. "Let's go show you how awesome the compound really is. We can walk, ride a bicycle, or take the car. Your choice." Corbin bent down and tied the lace to his shoe.

"I think I would like to walk." It was a beautiful fall day, and I needed as much exercise as I could get after I saw how fast Troy was.

"Excellent choice. I think you'll love it here."

We walked out of his house and down the gravel driveway. I smelled the flowers in the cool fall breeze. The wind blew through the trees, causing the leaves to make a rustling sound, and it was heaven to my ears.

Children's' laughter in the distance made me smile. I felt at peace here. If only Krista was with me. My stomach ached at the thought of her and what that monster was doing to her. I quickly brushed it away.

I would save her if it was the last thing I did.

We turned down a brick-paved road. There were several market places along the way, with everything from clothing to restaurants. It reminded me of the fair. Venders of all sorts aligned in their trailers.

I breathed in the scent of Mexican food, and my stomach let out a loud growl. My breakfast had worn off.

"That smells divine." I looked around all the food trucks to find the source.

"Ah, well then, let me introduce you to my father." He grinned and walked me over to a little white food truck.

"Hello, son, what brings you by today?" asked a man with dark curly black hair as his eyes settled on me. He grinned.

"Dad, I would like to introduce you to Jaime Weaver." Corbin pointed at me then pointed back at his father. "Jai, this is my father, Alan."

"It is a pleasure to meet you, Jaime. Are you kin to the Weavers here on the compound?" Alan asked, tilting his head to one side and getting a closer look at me.

"Yes," Corbin answered before I could reply. "Mary and Walter just confirmed she is Roberta and Jimmy's daughter."

"What? Where are they?" A smile lit up his face revealing ravishing white teeth. "Where have they been all these years?"

"We have recently learned they have been imprisoned for the last eighteen years, and we're going to try to rescue them," I said.

"Wow, well that is a lot to take in," he said. A line of customers was forming. "Kids, we can talk more later tonight in private." He passed us both a box of food and turned to wait on his next customer.

We found a picnic table to eat our wonderfully prepared meal.

"Corbin, this is delicious. I see where you get your cooking skills." I crammed the spicy fajita in my mouth.

"Thanks, he loves to cook." He, too, stuffed his mouth full. "He and my mom divorced two years ago, and he took up cooking to distract himself."

"Is your mom still on the compound?"

"No, she and my little sister Mandi moved to California. They visit often, but mom wanted a career outside of the compound and my dad didn't"

"Wow, everyone is so happy, I can't imagine why she would want to move away from here. It's very peaceful." Children played hopscotch and jump rope on the sidewalk, while others sat under trees reading or having picnics on the ground. "I feel like I'm in one of those 1950s commercials where the mom pops out this elaborate dinner and looks like she just stepped out of a magazine."

"I think that's what she hated most about it. She said it was too perfect. Electronics are limited here. We focus more on personal training and imagination.

"Mom enjoyed her computers and electronic devices," Corbin said. We finished our meal and resumed our walk. "We have televisions and games, but they are not used much." We walked up to three large brick buildings.

He pointed to each as he explained their functions. "This one in the middle is our court house. It's where most of the Elders live and conduct legal business. To the right, we have our teen and adult training building, and to the left is our school and children's training area."

"We all have jobs to help maintain the compound. We don't need money here because we all work so well together. And we're safe beneath the protective wall. It works as a shield of sorts. No one, unless invited in, can enter. There are fake gates used for visuals only.

"We are considered a gated community, so no one has ever attempted to enter unless they were lost. However, they usually gave up waiting for someone to answer our fake gate and drove away." Corbin pointed to different directions where the faux gates were located.

"From the air, it just looks like a small town. The elders handle land taxes, but everything else inside our compound is self-sufficient. We do own land outside the compound that is rented out and maintained by rental agencies. That's how we gain money for outside hunting expenses."

"I don't know what to say. It's amazing here." I thought about how different my childhood could have been, and it made the anger for Troy grow deeper inside me.

"Are you ready to start your training?" He snapped me out of my angry trance.

"Yes. I want to learn as quickly as I can, so I can get Krista and my parents back."

"Well, you will learn a lot, but we can't rush it. You must take your time and let your body learn on its terms." He stopped, took me by the shoulders, and made me face him.

"Okay, I understand. Let's get started."

We walked to the building on the right. It was the shape of an igloo, white brick with a large iron door. Corbin opened the door and took my hand as we entered the building.

"Just go with what I say, okay?" he whispered. "Folks are not too friendly to outsiders here." His words made me feel nervous.

The word 'outsider' echoed over and over in my head. I thought people would welcome me since I belonged to one of the founding families. Why did he want to keep that a secret? I supposed he had his reasons. I made a mental note to ask him to further elaborate later.

As we walked through the building, we approached a group of men who stood around a table playing a game of cards.

"Corbin, who is this very attractive young lady?" One of them asked—a guy with long, dark greasy hair.

My cheeks heated. No one had ever told me I was attractive before.

"What's up, Zane?" Corbin replied, as he threw his hand up and gave Zane a high five. "This is Jai, a friend of my sisters. Turns out she belongs to one of our outside clans." Corbin quickly walked passed Zane. "We're going to practice a bit. I'll catch up with you later."

I turned my head and saw Zane mouth the word, 'Damn!' It made me feel good that someone thought I was attractive. It was also funny to me, and I giggled.

"What is so funny?" Corbin asked.

"I don't know, it just tickles me that he finds me attractive, that's all."

"Well, I don't think it's funny. You're the most beautiful woman I've ever laid eyes on." He smiled at me.

My cheeks burned again, and I smiled back at him. Then I looked around. There were several different hallways with numbers above each entrance.

"What do all the numbers mean?" I pointed to them.

"Oh, those are for the ages. See, you learn more each year because your body gets stronger and it's able to tolerate more. So, each number represents that age group's training hall. Each hallway leads to a series of rooms. A physical training room for taekwondo and one-on-one combat, a workout gym, a mental clarification room, and a spell room. We'll start in the mental clarification room, so we can get an idea of what powers you might have. Then, we'll go into the gym for a workout. You'll need to strengthen your body and build up your stamina.

"Next, we'll move to the spell room to see if you can practice basic magic. Last, but of most importance, we'll begin learning the basics to taekwondo and self-defense. We'll do this in this order every day until you are ready." He winked at me, causing me to smile.

"I'll do anything if it gets me closer to my friend and my parents," I whispered.

We walked into an octagon-shaped room. There were several rooms within the room. Most of them were occupied and had people waiting on benches to enter once they were finished. We found an empty bench outside of a room marked with the letter A.

"What does the A mean?" I whispered in his ear.

"It means amateur," he paused.

My eyes widened.

"I'm teasing. They're just labeled for directional use. In case you're meeting someone to practice with."

I punched him on the arm and we both laughed.

A young woman with curly blond hair and beautiful blue eyes walked out of the room. She looked over at us and frowned. "Hey, Corbin, who is this chic?" She put her hand on her hip and pointed her finger at me with her other hand.

"Hello, Bethann. This is Jai, my friend." He stood up and jerked my arm, pulling me up with him.

"Hello," I said and stuck my hand out for a hand shake.

She rolled her eyes and pulled her hand away. "Corbin, really. It's been like two minutes since we broke up!" She huffed and walked away, shaking her bottom with every step.

Corbin laughed, turned toward me, and whispered, "It's been three years since we went on two dates. That woman is psycho."

"Remind me later what her super power is." I laughed and poked him in the shoulder with my finger. "That way I'll know how to defend myself when she decides she wants you back."

We walked into the empty room. It was painted a pale blue, and there was a desk in one corner with cards on it. There was also a sandbox with shapes and balls, a fish tank with plastic fish, and a table with candles.

"There are four elements in the universe. Earth, Air, Fire and Water. Each one of these areas works different abilities. The cards are for psychic abilities." He tapped his forehead. "The sand box with balls and shapes is for telekinesis. The fish tank is to see if you control the element of water, and the candles are to see if you can control the element fire.

"Wait, you mean five elements, right?" I asked remembering my mother's letter.

"I have only heard of four, but the Elders may know more about the fifth Element. We can ask them later. For now, let's focus on what I do know."

"Sounds like a plan. How does it all work?" I walked over to look at the card table.

"Some of us draw energy from the elements and some of us don't. Those who do can use this room to get stronger, and those who don't can use this room to keep hoping," he said as he pointed to each area.

"Like my little blonde friend over there. She only has psychic abilities and has been unable to control when she gets a vision. I think she tries too hard. Since we don't know what all you can do, we will start in here and move on as we go." He opened a small black notebook.

"Okay, it sounds like a good plan to me. Which one do we start with?" I was excited to see what I could do.

"Let's start with the psychic table." He pulled out a chair for me to sit down. I sat down, and he sat across from me. We each had a stack of cards. "Jai, I am going to hold up a card, and I want you to try to see what card it is using your mind. You will have to clear everything out and focus on the card." I closed my eyes and cleared my mind. I opened my eyes one at a time and stared and stared at the card.

"Nothing. I see nothing." But I already felt a little frustrated.

"Don't get irritated, just keep trying. Remember, this might be a gift and it might not be." He held the card up again. "Don't worry if it's not. Just try to let your body figure it out." Once again, I cleared my head and focused on the card.

"Nope, I don't see a thing." I let out a defeated sigh.

"Well, I don't have that gift, either." He laughed, and that made me feel better. We walked over to the sand box and sat down.

Corbin picked up a handful of sand. "See if you can do anything with this." I closed my eyes and blew hard. I managed to blow the sand right in his face. We both laughed, as that was no magical gift, but it was funny.

I tried again. I concentrated on the sand and it slowly spiraled up like a tornado. I gasped, causing me to lose focus and it fell. "I did that!!" I squealed with excitement.

"Yes, you did. It appears you draw energy from the Air element." He wrote in his notebook. "Now, see what you can do with these blocks."

I focused on the blocks, mentally making them stack on top of each other. One by one the blocks did just what I demanded them to in my head. "This is easier than I thought."

Corbin smiled. "This is just the beginning." He led me over to the fish tank. "See if you can shift the water slightly to one side of the tank."

I stood back and stared at the water. It was hard, because when I really concentrated on the water, it broke up into molecules. It was like I was seeing every drop individually. I was mesmerized by the beauty, and before I realized what I was doing, I had all the water out of the tank and swirling above our heads.

Corbin mumbled, "Wow."

I lost my concentration, causing all the water to crash down on us in a *whoosh*. We got soaked, and all we could do was laugh hysterically.

"Well, Water element, check." He attempted to write in his soggy notebook. "Just a thought—do you think you could put the water back in the fish tank?"

"I can try." I concentrated and watched as the droplets floated back into the tank, leaving us dry. Even his handy notebook.

"Amazing!" Corbin said as he pulled out his now dry notebook. We had one more to try. I sat down at the table with the candle.

"What do I do?" I asked as I stared at the white candlestick.

"Think about lighting the candle."

I concentrated and stared at the tiny wick. Nothing. I took a deep breath and tried again. Still nothing.

"Let's try this." Corbin made the flame come to life with a single bout of air.

I looked at him in astonishment.

"That's nothing compared to your water abilities." He chuckled.

"What do you want me to do with it now?" I asked as the flame danced in the shadows.

"Try to manipulate the flame." He pulled up a chair and sat beside me. "See if you can make it get bigger or if you can hold the flame in your hand."

"Are you crazy? I'm not holding fire."

"Don't worry. If you harvest the element of fire, it won't burn you when you're in control. You might feel some warmth, but do not fear it."

I focused on the flame, and it started to get bigger and bigger. I opened my hand and imagined the flame coming to me. It did just as I wished. I held the fire in my hands and it didn't burn. I tossed the ball of fire from one hand to the next before I sent the flame back to the candle and blew it out.

"I can't believe this is all real," I said as I stared at the unlit candle. "That was so incredible."

"It is amazing how fast you are revealing your abilities." Corbin took out his notebook again. "It usually takes weeks to develop a skill. It's a very good thing, too, given our situation. The ability to manipulate fire, but inability to attain it. Interesting," Corbin mumbled and jotted down the information. "Well, I think it's time to go change into our workout clothes."

I found the ladies' locker room and went in to change. It was clean, and each locker had a lock with a key in case someone wanted to secure her belongings.

Corbin had packed each of us a bag with snacks and clothes earlier. I pulled out my clothes and a bottle of water. I was a little nervous about hitting the gym. I had never stepped foot in one.

I changed clothes and stepped out of the locker room to wait for Corbin. The gym was set up with machines on one side and free weights on the other.

"Today we are going to work those pretty legs of yours," he teased, as we walked over to the treadmill. "We'll warm up here, then it's off to squats. A lady's best friend."

"I assure you none of this is very friendly." I was already getting out of breath on the treadmill. When that torture was over, we managed to do about thirty squats, twenty-five lunges, and we jumped up on a box. I still don't know what that did, except it almost made me bust my bottom several times. We had worked out for an hour, and I was sweaty and exhausted.

"Corbin, I am in desperate need of a shower and food." I retied my sweaty red hair into a messy bun on top of my head.

"Okay, not too bad for a first day." He held my sweaty hand and led me out of the gym. My heart skipped a beat every time he touched me. "Tomorrow, we'll start off in the spell room, then taekwondo, and of course we'll end in the gym."

We walked home, and I thought my knees were going to give out on me several times along the way. Corbin took a shower, then he called to talk with his father while I soaked in the Jacuzzi tub.

I ran the water and sprinkled in some of the rosewater bath salts. The smell was relaxing as the soft jets and warm water eased my tired muscles. I got out of the bath and put on a pair of cotton shorts and a tank top.

Corbin was in the kitchen, cooking. "Want some help?" I asked in a flirty voice.

"Sure," he replied and then he taught me how to make his grandparents' secret spaghetti. It was fun slicing vegetables and boiling noodles with him.

I enjoyed his company. He made me laugh a lot, which I desperately needed. We ate the amazing dish and cleaned up the kitchen. Afterward, we went into the living room and sat down on his brown leather couch.

"Do you like to play card games?" he asked.

"I only know how to play a few." I grabbed a soft brown cover and placed it on my lap. "I never really had anyone to teach me."

"How about UNO?"

"Oh, yes, I have played that one before." I smiled.

He pulled open a drawer of the coffee table and set up the game for us. It was so much fun. I never had that much fun with anyone except Krista. My mind wandered to her again. We put away the cards, and I teased him about losing.

"I won, by a long shot." I smarted off.

"You just wait, that was beginners luck." He put the cards away. "I'm going to kick your butt next time." Then he tickled me on my stomach. I squirmed my way onto the floor laughing.

I was worn out, and that incredibly soft bed was calling my name. He helped me up off the floor, and we hugged each other goodnight.

"Thank you for helping me, Corbin." I looked up and into his eyes as we released our hug.

"Jai, I have never met someone so determined and loyal in my life. It is my pleasure to help you any way I can," he whispered.

His breath warmed my nose. Our faces were so close. I wanted to grab him and let him see how I felt about him, but instead I pulled away.

"Thank you for that." Was all I managed to say. We turned all the lights off and went to our rooms for the night.

I climbed in the bed and felt sick to my stomach as I realized I was in a comfortable bed and Krista was probably scared and going through who knows what. I couldn't stop the tears from flooding my eyes. I knew I had to save her soon.

I woke up at seven in the morning and headed to the kitchen to make coffee. Corbin was already up and had breakfast waiting for me. Man, that guy was a morning person and loves to cook breakfast.

"Good morning," I said, as cheerfully as I could, given it was early and I needed my coffee.

"Good morning, beautiful," he said and sat a plate of food in front of me. I gobbled it up quickly and began cleaning the dishes while he worked on some paperwork.

"Did you sleep well?" he asked when he was finished.

"Like a baby." It dawned on me again that I didn't have my nightmare anymore and I was thankful.

"Good, because I'm going to kick your butt in taekwondo today." He dried the plate I had recently washed.

"Well, that's very likely. I usually run from confrontation, but that is a thing of the past." I playfully punched the air with both my hands.

"I'm teasing, we'll go easy on you today." He slapped me on to the bottom.

I jumped. I wasn't expecting it, and I laughed because it was funny, and I secretly enjoyed it.

We got to the training room by eight-thirty and went on into the spell room. The building was empty.

"Where is everyone?" I looked around at the empty rooms.

"It's hunting day, and I've decided I need to stay back and help you."

We walked into the spell room. It was painted a pale yellow, making the room appear bigger than it was.

There were herbs of all kinds lined up on shelves along the wall. There was a bookshelf full of different leather-bound books. Corbin grabbed a book off the lower shelf, opened it up, and sat it on a large center island table. Its pages looked old and delicate.

"Shouldn't we have on gloves?" I looked at the worn pages.

"No, these pages are stronger than they appear." He continued to flip through the book.

"What do they say?" I tried to read the book over his shoulder.

"These spells are simple. We'll start with them to see if you can practice original magic. If you can't, that's okay, too. It just means you only draw from the elements. The only way to know what you can do is to try everything."

I needed that gentle reminder. It bolstered my confidence. Then I read the first page aloud. Corbin placed a pot of soil in front of me.

"Should I like wave my hand around or something?" I asked, not really understanding what I was supposed to do.

"Nope, just concentrate on the seed and repeat the incantation three times." He instructed.

From the dirt, one may grow,
How, no one must know,
Rise and bloom,
To brighten this room.

I repeated it three times and watched as a seed began to slowly sprout and grow into a beautiful yellow rose.

"Wow! I can't believe I did this. It's all just overwhelming and exciting at the same time." I sat and allowed the moment to sink in.

"I'm sure it is. I can't imagine how you are feeling learning that you have had this power locked inside you all these years.
I was raised knowing what I am and all about magic. To learn now that you are older must

be frightening. I also realize it's a lot to take in at once." He sat beside me and took my hand. "I'm sorry you're having to find out this way. I know it's not easy."

"It's not that. I just keep thinking if I had these gifts growing up, maybe my life would have been much better." I sighed.

"Just remember, you are who you are because of your life experiences. You might not be the incredible person you are today if it played out differently." He kissed my hand, sending tiny shivers up my arm.

"I suppose that's true. What's next?" I took a deep breath and exhaled loudly. We worked on several other spells with success.

"We can note that you also have original magic to your list of abilities. Now, off to taekwondo."

We walked into the large room. There was a big mirror the entire size of the wall on one side and a blue mat on the floor. Several trophies were placed on a shelf in the back. There was what looked like a leg stretching machine and a punching bag near the back as well. A blond-haired man walked up to me.

"Hello, I'm Shaun." He offered his hand for a handshake. His eyes were hazel, and he had prominent dimples on both cheeks. He was about the same height as me five-feet, five-inches to be exact.

"Pleasure to meet you. I'm Jai." I shook his hand.

"Corbin has told me a lot about you. So, you've never taken any type of self-defense classes before?" Shaun asked.

"Nope, I'm not much of a fighter. However, certain circumstances require the trade." I smiled to let him know I was ready to learn.

He began by teaching me the tenants of taekwondo and how to become more comfortable screaming, as predators tended to run from loud encounters. It also alerted others that assistance was required.

It felt weird yelling for no reason, but I did as he said. We then practiced jump kicks and punches. He had to keep reminding me not to tuck my thumbs into my fists. We practiced for what seemed like hours.

Shaun was very patient with me and was good at helping me when my feet didn't want to cooperate with my brain.

We followed the same routine, day in and day out, for over a week. Shaun explained the color belt system to me. It's likely to take me years to achieve my black belt, but he says I am well on my way. I was getting faster, stronger and more confident each day.

Chapter Seven
HOME SWEET HOME

The day had come to move into my parents' home. It had been repaired, cleaned, and stocked with food. I was extremely excited, but I wasn't ready to leave Corbin. I had grown so attached to him the last twelve days, and the thought of being alone was overwhelming.

"Corbin, can I ask you a favor?"

"Of course, you can. What's bothering you, beautiful?" He walked over to me.

"Well, I know my home is ready, but I'm really nervous. I know there is this room I'm supposed to find, and I'm supposed to be so excited, but I'm not ready to leave you." I blurted it all out like one long, connected sentence, all the while tears flooded my face.

"Hey, love. Don't worry. I'm not leaving your side. I'm coming with you. The truth is, the more I'm with you, the more I want to be with you. I can't get enough of you, sweet Jaime Weaver."

I looked up at him and met his gaze. My heartbeat raced. His lips were so close to mine, all I had to do was lean in. Instead, we stayed still, inches from each other, breathless. I knew what I wanted, but I was so afraid of attaining it.

The doorbell rang and snapped us out of what could have been a truly magical moment. With a flushed face, I opened the door revealing my grandparents.

"Good afternoon." Grams smiled at me and dangled keys in front of my face. "I have the keys to your new house."

"We should head over there as soon as possible." Corbin handed me a black leather jacket out of a coat closet.

"If there is a secret room in that house, the construction crew was unable to locate it," Grams said. "Also, the scouts have come back bearing an unpleasant message for you."

My stomach knotted, and my throat constricted in fear that something had happened to Krista.

"What is the message?" I grabbed my Grams hand tightly.

Gramps opened a piece of paper and read from it. "If you do not deliver the amulet by sunset Friday, they will drain your friend Krista dry, along with the other fifteen scouts they captured."

"If it's the amulet I think it is, we haven't seen that since your mother disappeared." Grams walked over to get a look at the note. "It was a gift, but we never found out who gifted it to her. It was said to contain the fifth element, Aether. Your mother was convinced she was able to capture demons and send them to other dimensions using it."

"That's what your mother was talking about in her letter, the fifth element?" Corbin looked over at me.

"Mom mentioned that it merged with me somehow. Is that possible?"

"I'm not sure, dear. Aether is not noted much in our archives. Therefore, we know very little about it. Roberta did some research and said it can open other dimensions or speed up and slow down time by creating ripples. She was convinced she could do this while wearing the amulet. We must find it." Grams tone revealed her urgency.

All I could do was stand and listen. The bubble in my throat swelled, and I couldn't speak. What if I couldn't find the amulet? I didn't want to face that thing again, but I knew I must be strong for Krista.

"No time to waste. Let's go, Jai. We can get our things later." Corbin pushed me out the door.

"I'll meet up with you later," Gramps said, his voice sad. "I have to go explain the situation to the families of the missing scouts."

We jumped in Mary's little blue Toyota truck and headed to the Weaver plantation. I stared out the window, but my mind was focused on Krista. When we got to my new home, I burst out of the vehicle clutching the house key tight in my hand.

The house was even more beautiful up close.

"Your grandfather built your mother and father this house after they got married," Grams said as she walked up the steps.

I placed the key into the lock and opened the door. We all walked in and were greeted with a fresh breeze, courtesy of an open window, which allowed the scent of fall to welcome us.

Tears welled in my grandmother's eyes. "I just miss her so much." She placed her hand over her heart.

I patted her back to try and ease her pain as I looked around. The floors were white marble, and the walls were painted a light shade of gray, allowing the open floor plan to look even larger than it was. The spiral iron staircase leading to the second floor looked inviting, but my heart pulled me in a different direction. I walked down the long hallway.

There was a room to my left that contained a bed and a dresser, but it wasn't where my heart was leading me. I kept walking to the next door on my left, and I opened it to find the room was set up for a baby.

That baby was me.

The room was painted a precious rose pink. White curtains laced with pink flowers framed the wide windows. A wooden rocking chair accented with a dark rose-colored cushion sat in the corner, waiting for a rider who would never come. And the closet was full of clothes that were never worn. It was all set up beautifully for me.

I pulled out one of the dresses and held it in my hand. It was so tiny. Why did this happen to me? Why couldn't I have had the life my parents wanted me to have. Emotion flooded my mind and I couldn't hold back my tears.

I walked over to the dresser and opened the top drawer. There was an encryption on the inside that I couldn't read. "What does this mean?" I waved my hand to motion my grandmother to come inspect my findings.

Grams and Corbin rushed over to see what I was talking about.

"That's an old language we haven't used in decades," Corbin said, then he moved out of the way for my grandmother to see.

"To find what you seek, you must explore where the baby sleeps," she read.

We all rushed over to the baby crib and began inspecting it for any clues.

I pushed it out of the way, so we could get a better look at the side facing the wall, where we found a small outline. At first glance, it just looked like a hole or damage to the paint.

I squatted to get a better view. I knew that shape. I pulled off my bracelet to see if it matched. The initials fit perfectly. I placed the bracelet to the hole, and the wall slid open and revealed the secret room. Inside, maps, books, and potions were scattered about.

"It looks like they left in a hurry." Corbin said and picked up some broken glass.

I walked over to a baby blanket rolled up on the floor. When I picked it up, a necklace fell out.

There it was, the famous amulet that meant life or death to my friend... and perhaps the only thing leading me to my parents.

"Grams, here it is." I held the end of the silver chain attached to the oval-shaped turquoise amulet. It wasn't what I was expecting, but I had a feeling it was in fact what we are searching for.

"This dainty necklace caused all this mess?" Corbin took the amulet from me and inspected it.

"How do we find this monster? I have a fight to pick with him," I said, fury lacing my words.

"We can't just march in there hot-headed with no plan, dear," My grandmother said.

"She's right. We need to sit down and find out everything we can about this amulet." Corbin started searching through the scattered books. "Your mother did research, so that means she has information in here somewhere. We just need to find it. Mary, can you go get Walter?"

"Yes, I can. Please call if you find something." She gave me a pat on the back and walked herself out.

While she was gone, we went through journal after journal. I read each line of my mother's beautiful handwriting. My throat felt dry and my chest tight as read my mother's written words from her childhood throughout adulthood. My eyes welled with fluid and I allowed the tears to fall.

Even though she didn't raise me, I had a feeling I was very much like her as I looked at the organized room. Tried and tested spells neatly outlined in books. Potion fails, and demon sightings were placed in organized bins on a desk.

The thought of me being like her put a smile on my face for the first time since I found the amulet. But it didn't last long. We were getting tired and feeling desperate for anything that even resembled useful information.

"Here!" Excitement surged through me. "Look. This one is dated one month before my birth." I opened the book wider for us to read together.

I was given the most beautiful gift today but do not know whom I should thank for such a lovely offering. A necklace with a blue stone in the shape of an oval. I love it, but I feel there is something powerful about it. I fear there is more to this amulet than beauty.

Three days later...

Today, while wearing the amulet, I found myself in the future. I saw my end. I saw my child die at birth. I will stop this future from happening. I must! We will not die in our own home. I will not risk my unborn child's life. We will leave our home never to return. Jimmy thinks it's just my hormones. But I know it's not.

One day later...

I was once again forced into a future image of myself. This time Jimmy was pulled in with me. He saw our death. He felt what the amulet can do. We decided to start hunting the things in our vision.

We learned if we concentrate hard enough, we can trap the demons inside the amulet. They can't harm us. My research shows it contains the essence of Aether, which is why we can create ripples in time and see the future.

I am unsure if we are trapping the demons or sending them into another dimension. We need more time to figure this out. The baby is getting close. Mother says maybe another three weeks. Soon we will be unable to return home.

Three weeks later

We have confirmed that we are only sending the demons to another dimension. We also rescued several of our compound members. They were draining them of their energy. Something about opening the portal. They need this amulet to open it.

I have seen the future, and it has since changed. They will still capture us, but I have devised a plan to keep my child safe. They won't kill us. They want us alive, so they can drain us.

Since we both draw energy from the elements, they could keep us for some time. I only pray someone finds us. No, no, the baby is coming. She can't be born here. We must leave. Mom, Dad, if you find this, please know I love you.

Until we meet again,

Roberta

"She knew what was going to happen. How would demons get in here? Isn't it protected?" My voice warbled as I tried to calm my fears.

"I'm not sure. Didn't you mention she said there was a cosmic shift the night you were born?" Corbin asked.

"Yes, that's what my original letter said from her. Do you think that had anything to do with it?"

"Perhaps, if it can open and close portals. And if that's the case, maybe we need to keep it wrapped up, so our skin can't touch it."

"Wait," I said. "If they want the amulet, and we want our friends and family back, perhaps we can use it to our advantage. I have a plan."

My grandparents showed up moments later. We explained everything we had discovered and handed over the journals to them.

"I have devised a plan. We will deliver the amulet, but only on our terms. They must bring my parents, Krista, and all our scouts in exchange for the amulet. They are drawing energy from my mom and dad, who are now fragile. The demons need this amulet or one or more of us to survive. I don't think they can survive on their own without syphoning energy from someone. If we catch them in their diminished state, we may stand a chance." As the plan took shape, my hope grew. Maybe I could get them all back—Mom, Dad, Krista, and the scouts.

"I don't know, Jai. If they get you or that amulet, we're all doomed." Gramps piled the books up into a box.

"Oh, they won't get me, I assure you of that. If there is one thing I learned in the system, it's how to be sneaky and survive. And Corbin is blessed with strength. Once we get sight of our family, Corbin will crush this amulet, rendering it useless. Then, we fight and send those demons back to hell where they belong."

"It might work," Grams said. "We will need to plan a little more than that, but I believe you are on to something, my dear."

"Let's all sleep on it and discuss it first thing in the morning," gramps said.

We all agreed and said our goodbyes for the night. After my grandparents left, Corbin and I decided to tour the house before bed.

Finally feeling a little more upbeat about the situation at hand, I loosened up a bit. We ran from room to room playing hide and seek.

I decided to hide in the master bathroom shower.

He really wasn't very good at the game. I had to keep whistling to send him clues of my whereabouts.

Then he snuck up on me and yelled, "Gotcha!"

I jumped, punched him on the shoulder, and then laughed. "You scared the crap out of me." Then, seeking revenge, I turned the shower on and sprayed him with cool water.

He grabbed the shower head and sprayed me back. It was so much fun to just relax and be myself. We laughed at each other a long while, and I only stopped when my cheeks got sore.

"It feels so good to have hope again. I really think this might work."

"Yes, it is nice to have hope." He looked down at me and put his finger on my nose to catch a droplet of water. His touch made me feel nervous and excited at the same time.

We were focused on each other. I was mesmerized by his blue eyes and couldn't look away.

He raised his hand and brushed a wet curl from my face. As he did, he bent down and pressed his lips to mine. His arms pulled me into a strong embrace, and I lost myself in an amazing kiss. As we pressed ourselves closer together, he moaned, allowing his tongue to move freely with mine. My body ached for his touch, but I was afraid to go any further. It took every ounce of effort I had to pull away.

"Jai." He panted and ran his hand through his hair. "I am so sorry. I just couldn't hold it in any longer. Please don't be upset."

"Don't be sorry. I think we're great together. I just need to make sure we go slow. I'm not used to this."

"Used to what, exactly?"

"You know, boys and kissing and stuff." My cheeks burned.

He just laughed. "It's okay. I'm not, either. That was my first kiss."

"Seriously?" His confession both surprised me and warmed my heart. "You mean you never kissed Miss blonde headed fancy pants?" I teased.

He just grinned and nodded 'no' to me.

"Well, aren't we a pair?" I said.

"Let's go get changed into dry clothes and figure out our sleeping arrangements. We have a lot to do tomorrow." Corbin pulled off his wet t-shirt, reveling his bare, muscular chest.

I wanted to touch him so badly. "I know we talked about taking it slow and all, but would you mind sleeping in the room with me, fully clothed of course. It's just that it's strange here, and I don't want to be alone."

"I would feel much better being in the same room with you, but could you wear sweat pants and a t-shirt?" His face turned red. "I don't think I'll be able to control myself if you wear that satin nightgown."

"As long as you put on a shirt." I laughed and grabbed the ugliest pair of jogging pants in the closet. We picked the master room. It had a large king size oak bed where the other rooms had queen or twin beds. We climbed in and snuggled together, my head on his chest and his arms around me. Listening to his steady heartbeat lulled me to sleep.

The temperature dropped significantly, and I bolted up. I was no longer in the room with Corbin. I was somewhere else. A deserted park somewhere I'd never been before. The wind blew, and in the distance, the chains of a swing set squeaked. Darkness enveloped me, and the fog covered the ground like a blanket of white cotton. I rubbed my arms, attempting to calm the chill bumps that had emerged. Then I started exploring my surroundings.

"Hello!" I called.

No one replied, but a low humming sounded in the distance, so I walked in that direction. Someone sat on a park bench, but I couldn't tell who.

"I know you can see me, dear" the person said, in a scratchy deep voice.

"Who are you?" I looked around, trying to figure out where I was.

"I, my dear, am the void. I am what you all want. What you are all searching for."

"I'm only looking for my family and my friend. I don't even know what you are. I assure you, I'm not searching for you."

"Oh, but you are. You see, you are more like me than you know. Your mother, she knows what you are. One day, you will see, too."

"Stop with the riddles. I want to go back home. Why am I here?" My voice echoed in the distance.

"You are here, dear, because I need you to be here. I need you to see something of importance."

Although, I was frightened I walked closer to get a better look.

The thing or person was just a shadow—no face nor features, just darkness in the form of a hooded human silhouette.

"What is it I need to see?" I tried to sound stronger than I felt. Probably didn't succeed, though.

It lifted what would be hands to my temples and my mind clouded over. I had several visions.

One was of my mother in a room, sitting on a rusted metal chair. Her eyes were rolled back into her head, and she was attached to what looked like a very big battery. My father was not with her.

Then, the vision switched to Krista. She was crying and balled up on a rug on the floor. Her hands were stained with blood and her hair knotted around her face. She looked scared and cold. Hot tears rolled down my face.

The vision changed again. To me. I was holding up my hand, closing what looked like a gray tornado of sorts. Then the vision faded away. I didn't know what to make of it.

"What does that mean?" I took a step back from the creature.

"The first one is the past, the second one is the present, and the third one is the future," the Void said. "I had to know for sure if you were the one. When you were born, your mother was wearing a gift from our world, and somehow that power merged with you, child. You contain the power of Aether inside of you. With this power, you can open portals to other dimensions. You can create ripples in time, slow it down or speed it up. You can see the past, the present, and the future."

"Why are you telling me this?"

"I am telling you this because you will save the world from mass destruction. The demon holding your mother is very strong. He is an endolite demon. They are known for feeding off others' lifeforces. He is working to open the dimension of the dead to release every demon your mother and those before her sent there. If this happens, the world as you know it will be no more. You must not let him capture you. He doesn't know you contain this power, but he is smart. It won't be long before he figures it out."

The next thing I knew, I was back in the bed. Had it been real, or had it just been a dream? Uncertain and exhausted, I laid my head back down on Corbin's chest and fell asleep.

"Jai, it's time to wake up," Corbin said.

I sat up and wiped the crust from my eyes. My hair was frizzy and fluffed out all over the place. As I struggled to tame it, I filled him in on the dream I had. It had to be a dream. I mean, I was still in the bed.

"How would we know if it was real?" he asked as he helped me make the bed.

"I'm not sure, but Mom had written in her journal that she had seen the future.

Maybe if I concentrate hard enough, I'll see something, and that will verify the ability."

"Okay, let's try that after breakfast." He grinned about another delectable plate of food he had prepared for me.

I sat down at the breakfast table and looked around the lovely kitchen. Everything perfectly matched in shades of pastel yellow and light gray. The sunlight beamed in from an open window above the sink, allowing the smell of the sweet morning dew to fill the kitchen. We ate breakfast then headed to the compound for another round of training.

When we entered the training facility, I said, "I want to go see if I can tap into any future visions."

"I'll go ahead and hit the gym, and we can meet there afterwards."

We went our separate ways. I entered the room and locked the door, determined to make sure I had total silence and no interruptions. I lit the candle with a match and turned off the light.

The shadow of the flame danced along the wall. I sat on the floor with my legs crossed and closed my eyes, focusing on the future.

My heartbeat sped up, and the temperature in the room dropped. My head filled with fog, and when it dissipated, I saw my mother, crying. She was bent down beside my father, holding his hand. He was unconscious, but alive.

"Hold on a little longer, my love," she whispered between sobs. "Our baby girl is coming. I can feel her strength. She has found us."

Then, the vision faded away.

The next vision I had was of me holding a baby. I had a hospital band around my arm and was crying tears of joy. Then my head filled with black fog.

The last vision was of a graveyard. I stood before a gravestone, but the name remained unclear. Then, I snapped back to reality.

Well, that was jumbled up. How was I supposed to know what was past, present, and future? Or if they were all future visions, since that's what I was going for?

Obviously, I wasn't having a baby anytime soon, so there was that. However, it was good to see I had a future. The graveyard vision had me in knots, but I knew I must stay strong.

One thing for sure was that the void creature told me the truth. I could in fact see the past, present, and future. Perhaps once I learned to control it, it would be of significant use to me. I needed to speak to my grandparents about it further.

I blew out the candle and allowed the scent of the diminished flame to calm my nerves before I stood up and exited the room. Then I met up with Corbin and Shaun in the training room.

We followed the normal routine with taekwondo. My combat skills were getting better. I was already faster than Shaun. I never liked to fight growing up, but it didn't mean I didn't learn. I had a few 'scrappy street tricks' up my sleeve that they didn't know about.

"You are getting really good, Jai." Shaun tapped out for the third time in a row. "I'm not sure if you're a fast learner or if you're just naturally gifted in combat."

"Do you promise you aren't just letting me win?" I helped him stand up.

"I promise. I wouldn't be sweating like this if I let you win. I honestly believe you could take on most of the men in the compound." Then we bowed and shook hands.

"I agree," Corbin said. "I'm going to make sure to stay on her good side from now on."

We all shared a chuckle.

"We have to go meet up with the Elders," Corbin said. "Shaun, I'll call you later to fill you in on the plan." And we headed out the door.

My grandparents met us in a conference room just outside the training hall. The room was connected to all the age group hallways. It was massive in size and had shelves from floor to ceiling piled with books along each wall. A library ladder rested in the corner, ready to roll along the wall so readers could reach any tome, no matter how high on the shelves. In the middle of the room sat a large wooden table encircled by twenty chairs.

We sat together at the table as we ate our lunch and tried to decipher the maps from the house. I explained my vision with the Void and the other ones I had—except for the one with the baby. That one could wait for a more private meeting with Corbin.

Chapter Eight

UNCLE JONATHAN

"Well, that tells us two things for sure," Corbin said. "Your mother is alive, and they need her energy."

"For what, though?" I asked. "I mean these things were strong before they captured my parents. They had to be stronger than them to capture them in the first place. So, why would they need more energy? Unless, my previous theory is correct, and the demons can't live without steeling others' lifeforces."

"I'm not sure, dear," Grams said.

I stood up to walk around the room for a while, antsy as I thought about those things feeding off Krista.

"How do we find this thing in the first place? Did the messenger have details?" I kept pacing.

"I was so jumbled up, I don't remember." Grams fumbled through her purse looking for the crumbled piece of paper. "Ah, here it is. 'Jaime is to meet me at the Silverstone Deli before sunrise on the twenty-ninth of October.'"

"The twenty-ninth? That's tomorrow! We need to get our crap together and have a true plan tonight." I said with a sharp tone not meaning to sound rude, but we were running out of time.

"Excuse me, Jai. I need to speak with you."

Not recognizing the voice, I looked around the room to find a short older man dressed in a brown suit with a matching beret on his head. His 1940's clothing made me suspect he wasn't from the compound. Again, I scanned the room, but no one else seemed to notice him.

"Who are you and how did you get in here?"

"I am Jonathan Logan, a distant uncle of your mother. I have been sent to aid you in the collection of your parents and friend."

"Who let you in here?" My voice grew louder each time I addressed him.

"Jai, dear, who are you talking to?" Grams asked as she looked around the room.

"Uncle Jonathan." But when I turned around, he had gone. "Jonathan, where are you?"

"I'm here," he answered.

"Where? I can't see you."

"I'm right in front of you." He slowly appeared out of thin air.

"Whoa!" I ran and hid behind Corbin.

"What's going on?" Corbin tried to pull me in front of him.

"Didn't you see that man appear out of nowhere?" I pointed my finger at Jonathan.

"What are you talking about?" Corbin looked around the room and under the table. "There is no man over there."

My grandparents started laughing.

"What's so funny?" Corbin and I said at the same time with a frustrated loud tone.

"It appears that you have also gotten one of your father's many gifts," Gramps said. "He could see ghosts, too. Jonathan used to visit him from time to time, teaching him valuable lessons."

"Don't be afraid, dear. Jonathan is on our side." Grams took my hand and led me out from behind Corbin. "He will be of much use to us."

"Okay. So, I'm a little freaked out about this whole ghost thing. I don't want this gift. Can I just give it back or something?" I tried not look at Jonathan.

"No," Gramps said. "You can tune it out once you learn to control it, but for now we need to know why Jonathan has come to pay us a visit."

"They only send him when there is trouble brewing." Grams stated.

"What news do you bring, old friend?" Gramps stared into the blank space in front of me.

"The demons are trying to open the doorway to the Dimension of the Dead. You must not let this happen. They are syphoning off energy from your parents and friends to accelerate the process. Which has made them very strong." He paused for me to convey the message to the group.

"Those who do not draw energy from the elements may not survive. They can regenerate as they draw from the elements. Those that cannot will die."

As I passed his message on, I realized Krista couldn't regenerate. My blood ran cold through my veins. "What am I supposed to do? I can barely control my power, let alone battle some crazy-strong, energy-sucking demon."

"All you need to do is get there and destroy that amulet without getting caught," Jonathan said.

"Oh, yeah, simple enough. Especially the not-getting-caught part. Maybe it sounds easy for those who have trained their entire lives for this, but I..." I looked down at my hands, frightened at how little I could do, how little I knew. "I can barely complete a drop kick, let alone fight anyone."

"You can do this." Corbin grabbed my waist and pulled me back toward him. "You've already learned so much in such a brief time, and even Shaun is impressed with your fighting skills. Listen to your heart. It will guide your body through the actions you need to take. Just trust yourself."

I tried to take strength from his words and his embrace.

"Okay, time to get this plan put in place," Gramps said.

We spread the map on the table and decided to send some scouts to search the area to see if they saw anything unusual.

"I'll meet him at the deli, but I won't take the amulet." My confidence began to return. "Corbin will stay back and await my call. The only way this demon is laying eyes on that amulet is If I see my parents, Krista, and all the scouts he has in his possession. Then and only then do we bring out the amulet."

"What do we do if he doesn't comply?" Grams asked.

"Then I take my handy lighter out and torch the creep! I imagine his lovely followers are watching and waiting. I'm sure one of them will be more than happy to comply once their fearless leader is engulfed in flames."

"Well, you do make that sound easy," Corbin said as he bent down and plotted areas on the map. "You know it will never be that easy, right?"

"Yes, I know, but it's a start."

"Fine, so we do this, he tells us where to meet with the amulet, then what?" Gramps asked.

"Then we meet. But since I possess the power of Aether, we don't need the amulet. We crush it, and while he is distracted with fury, we kill him." I waved my hand like I was stabbing the invisible man.

"I don't think this is going to be as easy as you think, my dear," Grams said.

"Either way, I need to see Krista, and if it means I must fight, then so be it. I'll fight until I can't fight any longer if it means there's a chance I can save her." I slapped my hand down on the table for emphasis.

We all looked at each other and shook our heads in agreement.

I covered my uncertainty with false bravado. They were all trained well in magic and fighting, while I'd barely learned to control water and fire, let alone fight a power-hungry demon. But it all came down to me, and I had to get their buy-in on the plan. The only way to do that was to feign confidence. It was all I had to work with. I had to save my friend, my parents, the scouts. Even if it was with a half-thought-out, desperate plan.

We all parted ways. Corbin and I went back to the plantation and headed to the garden area. We walked through the double doors and were immediately hit with a gust of cool air. The leaves were scattered around from the swift wind. I pulled my zipper up on my jacket and made my way to a swing. The flower beds that once contained vibrant flowers were now just covered in leaves. There was a bird bath with no water and a seedless bird feeder in the middle of the yard, surrounded by cement benches.

I closed my eyes and listened to the leaves rustling in the wind. It was peaceful out there. I ran my plan over and over in my head. If I just let my heart guide me... The thought replayed over and over, but I had no idea what that meant. My heart told me a great many things, but how to fight wasn't one of them.

Corbin and I sat out there the remainder of the afternoon, rocking back and forth in the swing and not speaking a word. Tomorrow was the day. We may not survive, but I would do my best.

Corbin slept in the room with me again that night. I didn't feel as frightened when he was around. Funny how that was. Growing up in the foster care system, I was always terrified of men and certainly wouldn't trust one in my bed. But Corbin was different. He didn't scare me and certainly knew his boundaries, although sometimes I wished he didn't. I drifted off with the vision of me and my baby in my head.

At least that gave me comfort that I would survive this fight, and seeing me with a child, I believed Corbin would, too. What I didn't know was how far in the future that vision was.

Chapter Nine

FACE TO FACE

Time to meet the traitor I once called my friend. I didn't know what hurt me more—the fact that I trusted him or the fact that I let my friend near him.

I wanted to punch his glowing-eyed face into the ground for what he had done to us. For now, I decided to remain calm and allow him to think I was some weak-minded little girl with no strength. If it got me what I wanted, I'd play any role. But when the time came, he would be praying for mercy as I made him suffer in ways he never thought possible.

I felt something building up inside me, and a rage I'd never before known engulfed me. I looked into the mirror—I no longer recognized myself. My usual jade eyes glowed mustard yellow.

"Corbin!"

He immediately ran to my aid. "What's wrong?" He recoiled and pointed at my face. "What's going on with your eyes?"

"I don't know." I raised my voice and called out, "Jonathan!"

"Hello, Jai," he said, all too chipper.

"Please tell me you know what's wrong with my eyes."

"I sure do!" He clapped his hands together. "You, my sweet girl, are part werewolf. It's the reason you can see me. Canines, or those that are part canine, can see what the human eye cannot."

"Am I going to turn all hairy and smelly? Why didn't my grandparents tell me about this?" I began to freak out. My breathing was fast as I was close to a panic attack.

"Only if you want to. Calm down, Jai. Take a deep slow breath and exhale slowly."

As if.

"They probably didn't tell you because half-breeds can't shift, or none that we've ever seen could. They are only able to see ghosts. I'm not exactly sure why you are able to do it. The only thing about being in wolf form is you can't use any other magic. Those abilities only work when you're in human form," he explained.

"What use is my wolf form, other than letting me see ghosts?"

"You will have more strength than usual as a wolf. You will also be able to find things or people with your enhanced sense of smell. With practice, you can do these things in your human form when you channel your wolf side."

I continued relaying the information to Corbin as I tried to process everything Jonathan said.

"You must use caution, however, because if you channel your wolf side too much, you will fully transform and have no magic. It's a delicate balance, and your emotions are the trigger points."

"So, when I feel fear or anger, my wolf side will emerge?" I wasn't sure I fully understood.

"Precisely!" He clapped his hands again.

"Then it's a good thing I've learned to control my temper over the years." I smiled, then I looked at Corbin who was staring at his feet. He had a concerned look on his face.

"Jonathan, will you leave us for a moment, please?" I asked.

"Yes, ma'am." He disappeared.

"Corbin, does this change how you feel about me?" My nerves went crazy in my body.

"No. It's just that I worry about you, and now there's this additional aspect. If you lose focus and transform, you won't be able to protect yourself from their magic. I just want you to be careful."

As much as I wanted to tell him not to worry, I knew that would not calm either of our fears. "I promise I will do all I can to stay calm. I'll just think of how cute and fluffy I'll be when I go all doggy on that creep." My gentle teasing lightened the mood, and we both laughed.

"Now it makes sense why he calls you 'little wolf' all the time." Corbin fluffed my hair with his hand.

"What I don't understand is how he knew."

"I'll leave you to finish getting dressed. Mary and Walter will be here soon, then we'll all head to our destinations." Corbin planted a kiss on my forehead. "Just remember—stay calm and stay alive for me."

I pulled out a pair of black leather pants and a black turtle neck. Both had been infused with some sort of protection spell by my grandmother. Apparently, that style of clothing is what the Protectors wore when they went on hunts. I laced up the combat boots and took one last look at myself in the mirror. I looked pretty good. If anything, maybe I could impress Troy with my figure.

It was almost time. My grandparents were waiting for me. I inhaled a deep breath and slowly exhaled, attempting to calm the butterflies in my stomach.

There was a knock at the door, then Shaun and Alan came in.

"You didn't think I was letting you do this on your own, did you?" Shaun patted me on the back. "I'm coming with you."

"Shaun, are you sure?" I gave him a huge hug. It meant a lot knowing he would stand and fight beside me.

"I won't let my favorite new student get beat up by a worthless, power-hungry demon." He smiled. "I am certain."

"Thank you." My watch beeped, letting me know it was time to leave.

Corbin handed me a cell phone and a pin that had four different triangles on it. One regular blue triangle facing down, one red-orange triangle, one green triangle facing downward with a horizontal line through the peak and one yellow with a horizontal line through the peak.

"What is this?" I asked as he pinned it to my shirt.

"My father did some research. This represents the four elements. Earth, Water, Air, and Fire. When combined, they form a star for the fifth element, Aether," He placed a kiss on my cheek. "It's to remind you that you are part of the universe, as it is a part of you."

"It's beautiful. Thank you." My voice cracked as I tried to contain my emotions.

"Thank my father." He pointed to Alan. "He made it for you."

"You are a brave and strong young lady," Alan said and gave me a hug. "You can do this if you believe in yourself."

This was only the second time I had spoken to Alan, but he seemed to be a gentle and loving soul. That explained so much about Corbin. My heart, and my courage, were fortified.

I took a deep breath and turned around. Then we all headed out of the compound to our set destinations.

The scouts we sent out returned empty-handed, but they remained stationed all over the city. Most them were around the deli in case I needed backup. Which was comforting to know.

Shaun squeezed my hand and reminded me to breathe. "Just remember, he needs that amulet. He won't hurt you until he has it, and you must not allow him to see you draw the power of the fifth element, or he won't need the amulet at all. He'll take you, instead."

"Duly noted." I opened the door to the deli and we entered.

Troy sat at the bar holding a short glass of gold-colored drink. He looked over at us and met my gaze. "Ah, how sweet, you brought a friend along. What's the matter, little wolf? Are you scared of little old me?"

"I'm not afraid of you. I despise you." The sight of him made me want to vomit. "He's here to help me with my friends, as I'm sure you've had your gritty fingers all over them."

"Enough. Where is the amulet?"

"Where are my friends and family?" I placed my hand firmly on my hip.

"Oh, they're far from here, little wolf." He sneered.

I wanted to slap his mirth right off his face. "That's too bad, because you're not getting the amulet until I have everyone back. Krista, my parents, the scouts... everyone."

"Don't toy with me, child. I'll rip you in half." He growled, and his eyes flickered crimson.

I smiled, because I had irritated him. It only enticed me to continue. "Go ahead and try. You'll never get your precious amulet if you do." I laughed to show him I wasn't scared. I was terrified, but no way was I going to let him know. "If you want your valuable amulet, you'll bring my parents, Krista and the other protectors unharmed to the park on Twenty-Third Street in one hour." I walked backward, bumping into the glass door on my way out.

His eyes glowed bright red. Part of me was proud that I held it together, another part thrilled that I made him so angry, but a third part—the biggest part—was chomping at the bit to get away from him.

We made it to the car without incident. Thankfully, Shaun drove, because my hands shook too much to control a car. I could barely get my seatbelt fastened.

"I did it! I managed to stay alive and call his bluff." Relief flooded through me.

"Don't get too excited, Jai. The hard part is yet to come," Shaun reminded me.

I called Corbin to let him know how the meeting went.

"That's wonderful news. I'll call the scouts to see if they can follow him. Maybe we can get lucky and find the location of that power supply."

"All the other scouts will be stationed around the park to assist us if needed. Mary and Walter will be close with healing potions and supplies for everyone." Shaun spoke loud enough so Corbin could hear, too.

"Jai, don't get too excited," Corbin said. "Troy will bring many friends with him. We must play this by the book. Remember, the second that amulet is crushed, you better be ready for impact, because he is going to unleash all hell on us."

"I know. I just wish I knew how to control my powers better. If I could, he wouldn't stand a chance. If we just had more time."

"That's what everyone says when times get tough, love. All we can do is hope your powers come naturally. Like an extension to your hand. Don't think too much, just feel and act. And we'll all be right there with you."

"I'll try my best. See you in half an hour." I hung up the phone. We arrived at the park in exactly thirty minutes, and the scouts took their positions.

The sky was full of clouds, the air thick with humidity.

"A storm is brewing." I pointed at the sky. Then I sat next to Corbin, cross-legged on the ground to meditate and calm the storm also brewing inside of me.

If I felt the elements, maybe my power would come more naturally. I reached my mind out into nature. One-minute I was sitting there, and the next I was in a vision. There was to be a fight. Corbin crushed the amulet, and glittering shards rained from his hand. Troy ran over and grasped him by the throat. His mouth gaped wide as he gasped for air. Troy had some sort of dagger with symbols on it. He plunged the blade between Corbin's ribs, seeking vital organs. Blood spurted from the wounds, then Corbin's body dried up. Something—I assumed it was his essence—was absorbed into the dagger.

No, no, no!! That cannot happen.

"Jai, wake up. It's almost time." Corbin shook me alert.

I came to, stunned to realize I was in the same place I was before the vision.

"Corbin, you have to go. Now!"

"I'm not leaving you"

"I've seen your death. He has a magical dagger that draws your entire soul into it. You must go. Please," I pleaded as I tugged on his jacket collar.

"I trust you, and I'll leave, if only not to distract you. But I'm not going far." He handed me the amulet. "If he lays one hand on you, I'm coming back."

My heart raced. All I wanted was for him to get to safety. Relief washed over me as I watched him leave.

I was thankful for the gift I was given of seeing the future. Hopefully I had manipulated the outcome. I stood there, holding the beautiful oval amulet. Its color glowed bright turquoise in my hand. I took in a deep breath and grabbed the chain that was linked through a hole in the top of the amulet. Once I let go of the amulet itself, it stopped glowing.

"Do you think that's a sign I harvest energy from it?" I asked Shaun.

"I'm not sure, but considering it only does it when you touch it, I'd say it's a pretty good indicator that it does. Once you touch that amulet, he is going to know. Unless you wear these." He pulled out a pair of black leather gloves and handed them to me. "I don't know if it will work, but it's worth a try."

I put them on and grabbed the amulet. I gave Shaun a high five. "Success!"

We saw headlights in the distance, indicating that they were almost here.

"Let's kick some demon butts and save our friends," I shouted, trying to pump myself up. My stomach was full of butterflies, and my hands were trembling.

"Shaun, if you get the chance, get that dagger from him, please." I knew I would be too distracted and he was fast maybe he could get it.

"I'm on it."

And we stood there, waiting and watching as the vehicles got closer and closer.

Corbin's mother, whom I'd yet to meet, his father, and the rest of the scouts were stationed around the perimeter of the park. Everyone was hidden ready to pounce if needed. Just knowing they were all out there gave me more courage as I waited for Troy.

Chapter Ten

THE EXCHANGE

I tried to stay calm and keep my fidgeting to a minimum. My heart was in my throat, and a mantra played over and over in my head—I could do it, I could do it.

I caught myself holding my breath when the vehicles came to a stop about a yard away from us. Troy got out of the car first and approached. Two tall, stocky men followed him, holding Krista by the arm.

"Where are my parents and the other protectors?" I asked.

"Caution, little wolf. It only takes one snap of my finger to crack your pretty little human's neck." He smirked.

Anger boiled up inside me, and my cheeks started to burn. Shaun moved closer to me, reminding me to stay calm.

"If you hurt my friend, you'll never get the amulet. You see, it must be given to you. You can't just take it from me. And right now, I don't feel very generous. I will ask only one more time. Where are my parents and the other protectors?"

I hoped he didn't call my bluff about the whole giving thing. I totally pulled that out of my ass. He nodded his head at the two men. They shoved Krista at me. She had a black bag around her head.

"Shaun, would you remove that awful bag from my friend's face and assure me she is unharmed." I wouldn't avert my gaze from Troy, wouldn't let my guard down.

"What's going on?" Krista yelled and struggled as Shaun removed the bag.

"It's okay, Krista," Shaun said. "I'm here with Jai. We are taking you home very soon." He radioed some scouts to come retrieve her and ordered another set to wait for the arrival of the rest of our group.

Troy brought three scouts at a time. Shaun inspected each of them from head to toe and led them away to safety. My eyes never left Troy. That amulet must be powerful for him to cooperate this fully with me.

My parents were the last two brought to me. I finally averted my gaze from Troy. My heart skipped a beat as Shaun removed the bags, revealing them to me. They were both frighteningly pale, and their faces were covered in bruises. Their clothes were ripped and stained with dirt and blood. I hated to think what their bodies looked like underneath their rags.

"Jaime, get out of here." My mother cried out loud." She attempted to turn around and face Troy.

"Shaun, get them out of here quickly." I growled as anger engulfed my body. He walked them to the scouts and returned to me.

I took a breath, reminding myself to stay calm while the scouts escorted them to safety.

Troy growled. "There, little wolf, you have all your useless friends. Now, give me the amulet."

"You mean this little thing?" I held it in front of my face.

"Yes, now hand it over."

"We have a problem," I said. "The deal was that my friends and family would be returned to me unharmed, and while many were, my parents were not. They are pale, emaciated, and banged up. What did you do to them?" I stalled as I worked up the nerve to crush the amulet. I knew I needed the strength of my inner werewolf to crush it, but I couldn't let myself go too far wolf in the process.

"It doesn't matter what I've done, mutt. I've got men all over this park ready to rip you all to shreds if you don't comply." His eyes glowed red.

"Mutt, huh? Let's not resort to childish name calling, Troy." I backed up and tried to stall. We needed more time for my grandparents to get everyone back to the compound safely.

"I'm only going to ask one more time before I make you feel so much pain you will have no choice but to hand it over." He sneered again.

At least I knew my little white lie worked. "I don't know... You see, it's because of you that I was raised in the foster system. It's because of you that I have never met my parents. Why should I just hand the amulet over to you?" I glared at him.

"Because if you don't, you and all your friends will add to my power bag. I'm not afraid of a little half-wit wolf. I'll take what's mine if I have to pry it out of your cold dead hands."

"I don't think that will be necessary." I smiled and held up the amulet.

He grinned and walked up to me, stood close enough for me to touch.

I smelled his foul breath as he said, "I knew you were too afraid to try anything stupid."

His words had me seeing red. It was just the push I needed. I crushed the amulet in his face and blasted him away from me with a single movement of my hand.

I'm not sure where the energy came from, but it was certainly welcomed.

He stood up to charge at me, his eyes full of hatred.

I jumped, just meaning to get out of the way, but my animal instincts kicked in and I landed on top of him. I wasn't fully wolf yet, but I was close. I punched then jumped off him, wanting to get as far away as I could. Out of the corner of my eye, I saw him pull the dagger out.

I shot another wave of wind in his direction, pushing him backward, causing him to drop the blade.

He launched a ball of flames at me.

I ducked and ran toward him. When I was close enough, I drop-kicked him, causing him to stumble to the ground.

He managed to punch me hard across my cheek, causing spots in my vision.

I fell to the ground, my jaw pulsing with pain, but I quickly forced myself up and attacked. I elbowed him in the neck.

He rained down a fury of blows to my face.

I reached up and raked my nails down his cheek, clawing for his eyes, then I jumped back just in time to catch a ball of fire. I threw it back at him, knocking him down again. My vision clouded, and I let my mind take over. A gush of energy soared throughout my body. It was exhilarating. The air around me began to spiral, pushing him further away from me. I held up my hand, causing him to levitate closer to the tornado that I had caused in the sky.

"You will not harm my friends or family ever again." My voice was an unrecognizable growl. I threw him into the tornado and fell to my knees, exhausted.

No one had explained I would be so drained after the battle. The air died down around me, and I saw several overturned cars and some playground equipment that was once cemented into the ground. I gasped, stunned I had caused such destruction.

Shaun stood beside me and helped me to my feet.

"Where is he? Did I kill him?" My body shook from fatigue.

"No, Jai, you didn't kill him. You did, however, manage to send him away from here. Which means he or his men will be back, and now they know you harvest energy from Aether."

"At least we managed to get everyone to safety before I lost control," I whispered and stared at my feet.

"Jai, don't be disappointed. You were amazing. I've never seen someone have that kind of power." Shaun walked me to the little white sedan. "The only thing is, now that they know, they will come for you. You'll have to be prepared."

"At least I have my parents to help me train." A yawn escaped me. I tried to rest on the journey back to the compound, but my thoughts were of Krista, my parents, and Corbin.

Shaun pulled up in front of my house— my parents' house. I didn't even wait for him to turn the engine off before I opened the door and ran inside.

Corbin met me at the entrance with open arms. "Jai, honey, you were amazing. How did you do that?" He wrapped me in his arms.

"I have no idea. I felt angry, and I took a breath to calm myself. The next thing I remember is Shaun helping me up. I faintly remember hearing myself speak, only it wasn't me. It was someone or something else speaking through me. Corbin, I'm frightened at what I am capable of when I lose control. I could have hurt someone." I pressed my face into his chest and breathed in his scent.

"It's okay, baby. We'll figure this out. But right now, I think there are a lot of happy people who want to see you. Brace yourself, though. Your parents are pretty weak and will require time to heal."

I got up and walked into the living room. My parents weren't in there, but my friend was.

Krista sat on the couch, wrapped in a blanket. Shaun had made her a cup of hot tea, but she pushed it aside when she saw me. She jumped to her feet and ran toward me, embracing me and nearly knocking me off my feet. "Jai, you found me!"

Tears rolled down both our faces. I pulled her back to inspect her for injury. "Are you okay?"

"Thanks to you. What was he?"

"I'm not sure. All I know is he's powerful and cruel. What did he do to you?" We sat on the couch and Shaun offered her the tea again.

"He took me to this place. Underground, I think. He had a bag over my face, so I couldn't tell where we went. It was damp and musty, though. And I could hear someone crying in the distance.

"It was a long walk before we reached the holding room. Once we got there, he took the bag off my head and untied my hands. Then he locked me in a small cage.

"The floor was dirt and the metal bars were peeling with yellow paint. There were several cages down there. A man and a woman were tied to chairs with weird, glowing helmets on their heads. It looked like it was feeding off them or something. They appeared to be asleep the whole time.

"It was freezing and smelled of dead animals. He left me alone for a while, then a few days later, he brought in more people and put most of them in the chairs, too. Others he threw in cages like mine."

"Oh, Krista. I'm so sorry."

She shook her head. "They brought in stale bread and water once a day. Sometimes they kicked us around, but that's about it. I don't know how the ones on the chairs ate. They never got any food or water that I saw. It was cold down there. I could hear what might have been a train in the distance. Oh, Jai, it was awful. They never spoke to us, but their creepy red eyes haunted my every dream. I can't believe Troy was one of those things."

Shaun covered her up, placed his arm around her, and patted her back, allowing her time to just let her frustrations out.

"I think a couple of people are eager to meet you." Corbin reached for my hand to lead me into the bedroom.

I stopped in the doorway and stared. Sitting on the bed were my parents.

My heart leaped with joy. I'd waited my entire life for this moment, although I had envisioned it much differently. I found myself speechless as I entered.

"Jai, you found us. I knew you would rescue us one day." Mom opened her badly bruised arms for a hug. I knelt beside the bed and gently returned the gesture.

"Are you okay? What did they do to you?"

"They syphoned our energy," Dad said, leaning over and joining in the embrace.

"They believe if they harvest enough energy, they can open the Portal to the Dead, bringing back every demon we've ever killed," Mom said.

"And he needed the amulet to complete the ritual?" I asked.

"Yes, that was the last item needed. And now that it's destroyed, and you've revealed your powers, he will come for you." Mom's eyes shone with tears.

"Well, I'm not going to let that happen," Gramps said as he entered the room.

"Neither am I," Corbin chimed in.

"Krista said you were connected to a chair that syphoned your energy. Do you know where that energy went?" I asked.

"Yes," Dad said. "There's a device much like a battery that's connected to the helmets. The energy is built up and stored in that container until the harvest ceremony."

"The harvest ceremony?"

"It's on All Hallows' Eve," Mom said. "It's the day they plan to open the portal."

"Which also means we need to prepare ourselves for war, because the only way they can open that portal now is with you," Gramps replied. "I'm going to let you guys catch up. Corbin can fill me in later." He nodded at Corbin and walked out of the room.

"Unless we could find that energy source and destroy or release it before then," Corbin suggested.

Dad sat up in the bed. "That might work, but we don't know where it is."

"Well, let's look at what we do know about its location. It's at least within an hour from the park. Krista mentioned hearing a train and that it felt like she was underground. We could look at a map and draw out a sixty-mile radius around the park, focusing on all the areas near a railroad crossing."

"That's a great idea, Jai. I knew you were going to inherit my brain," Dad said, and we all laughed.

"Speaking of inheriting things, you two are going to have to explain to me how all this stuff works, because I'm a hot mess, but full of pretty awesome powers that I have no idea how to control." I waved my arms around my body as I spoke.

"There will be plenty of time for that tomorrow," Corbin said. "Tonight, let's let these guys get some rest."

He was right. It had been a long time since they rested on their own bed. I gave them both a hug, closed their door, then turned to Corbin. "Where are all the others?"

"Walter and Mary escorted them all to their homes prior to your arrival, as their families were eager for their safe return. All thanks to you, little wolf." He tousled my hair.

"Well, to be honest, they wouldn't be in that mess if it weren't for me." I said.

"Not true. That amulet would have been given to someone eventually. It just happened to be your parents. By the way, Walter and Mary are going to come back here to sit with your parents tonight. I'll take you and Krista to my house. If that's okay?"

"Yes, that sounds great to me. Will it be okay for Krista to stay in the compound until this is all over? I know her parents are worried sick because I haven't contacted them again, but I don't know how to explain without sounding like a lunatic."

"Absolutely, she should stay here. They would all be at risk if she returned home now. It's probably best that they think the two of you are missing or still having the time of your life at some beach somewhere. Once this is all over they will just be relieved you both are safe. Let's just keep it from them a little longer. Anyway, I think Shaun is smitten with her."

We both looked in the living room and found Shaun and Krista sharing a laugh. It looked like Shaun was telling her jokes. I smiled, knowing whatever happened to me, she would be okay.

"Hey, Shaun," I called. "We're getting ready to head back to Corbin's house. Would you like to come with us?" I waggled my eyebrows at Corbin.

"Sure, that sounds like a plan to me." Shaun took Krista's hand and helped her up.

We were all exhausted, and I was an emotional roller coaster. One minute I was gawking over my friend's romance, then as those thoughts evaporated, I remembered that the monsters were still out there. It made my skin jump as the thought crossed my mind.

I'd cross that bridge tomorrow. Tonight, I needed rest. We arrived at the house, and I walked Krista in while the guys talked outside. I took her to the room I stayed in and showed her where to find everything.

"Do you want me to stay with you tonight?" I asked while I picked out a nightgown for her.

"Yes, please. I don't want to be alone," she said quietly as she started running the bath water.

"Then, I promise I won't leave your side." I stood at the bedroom door and called for Corbin.

"I'm going to stay with Krista tonight. She doesn't want to be alone. But would you please leave your door open in case we need you?" He was facing his bedroom door, so I stole a quick glance at his bottom before he turned to face me.

"I would walk through fire for you, Jai. I will most certainly leave the door open."

I was pretty sure I'd fallen in love with him. My stomach turned to mush every time he looked at me.

Shaun walked down the hall. "I'll leave mine open too, little lady," he said in a terrible attempt of a cowboy impersonation.

I laughed and gave Corbin a quick nod and closed the door. I hated being away from him, but I knew my friend needed me. I went into the bathroom and sat on the toilet while Krista soaked in the tub.

She had the curtain pulled so I couldn't see her, but I could hear she was crying. I pulled the curtain back to talk to her, and I recoiled when I saw the many bruises that covered her body.

"Oh, Krista, what did they do to you?" My heart ached for her. There were so many bruises.

"Nothing I can't handle. I'm just so thankful you found me. I don't think I would have lasted much longer in that place." She took my hand.

I was trying to be strong for her, but I couldn't hold back my tears. I vowed to make that demon pay for what he had done to her.

"Here, let me wash your back." I grabbed the body wash and wash cloth. Her entire back was covered in shades of yellow, black, and purple.

She hissed as I gently pushed the cloth around, and again I fought back tears. "There, nice and clean. While you wash your hair, I'm going to get Corbin to get you some ibuprofen to help with the pain and swelling. I'll leave the bathroom door open, so I can hear you." Then I walked back to the bedroom door.

"Corbin, can you get some ibuprofen and a glass of water for me, please?" I called out loudly.

"Sure thing." He was at the door in a flash. "I thought you two might need this, so I had it ready. How is she doing?"

"She says she's fine, but she's covered in bruises. I'm sure there are things she isn't telling me, but I know Krista. She'll let me know when she's ready. Thank you for the medicine." I gave him a quick peck on the lips and went back in the bedroom.

I set the medication and water on the night stand, grabbed a soft robe, and took it to the bathroom. Krista stepped out and donned the pink bathrobe. She sat down at a little white bench in front of the mirror, and I brushed her long raven hair.

Afterwards, we lay side-by-side in the bed talking and laughing about our childhood memories together. For that small amount of time, it was hard to forget everything that had happend, but we drifted off with happy thoughts.

Chapter Eleven

THE VOID WITHIN

"Hello again, Jai," a recognizable voice said. I turned my head to see the Void standing behind me.

"What is it you want with me?" I asked.

"It's not what I want. It's what you must do."

"What is it that I need to do, then?" My voice dripped with sarcasm. I was getting irritated by its riddled answers.

"You must allow me to help you fight the demons. You must give me permission to gain full control of your body when the time comes."

"What? No way you are hijacking my body."

"Jai, we both know you cannot control your powers and I can. You need me."

"I'll be able to control my powers with a little bit of practice. Wait a minute! It was you, that talked through me at the park, wasn't it?"

"It was. And I am the one who sent the demon away. I just didn't send him far. Perhaps a state over or something. Without your complete cooperation, I can't tap into your full power. You were fighting me tooth and nail the whole time."

"If I can learn to control my power, I won't need you. Who says I'll need you anyway?"

"It is essential that I help you. Let me show you something." It sighed and lowered its hood, revealing the face behind the shadow.

I gasped. "You—you're me. I mean, I am you. How is this possible?" Confusion muddled my thoughts.

"When you were born, there was a cosmic shift. Somehow that mixed with your mother's power to harvest from the other elements and caused a part of your essence to merge with the amulet. That resulted in you being born on this side, while I was born in the void. We are intertwined, you and I."

"If I let you have full control, how long will that last?"

"I will only take control when I am needed and leave when I am not. It's exhausting for both of us, therefore, we merge only in extreme circumstances."

"What happens after all of this is over? Do you just go back to the void?" I asked.

"I'm not sure. This has never happened before. All I know is I am a part of you, and you need me."

"Okay." She was right. I felt her strength and knew without a doubt I needed her.

"For now, you must continue training, so you can fight as much on your own as possible. We will have to save as much energy as we can to beat these things." And with that, she disappeared.

I woke in the bed with Krista sound asleep beside me. It had been another dream. How do I call on her? I'll have to ask myself the next time I saw myself in a dream.

What a muddled mess this turned out to be.

I got out of bed and stepped into the shower. I allowed the hot water to run down my face as I ran my dream through my head. When the water cooled, I climbed out and got dressed.

Krista still slept, but I didn't wake her. I imagined she needed as much rest to heal as she could get. I tiptoed to the door and whispered Corbin's and Shaun's names. I promised I wouldn't leave Krista's side, even though I knew she was perfectly safe. But a promise was a promise, and I was in desperate need of coffee. I also needed to fill them in about my dream session with my void side.

Corbin walked up, rubbing his eyes. He, too, looked like he had a restless night.

"Good morning, beautiful." He bent down to kiss my forehead. I loved that he could show me affection even though we weren't a real couple... yet. I welcomed every sweet gestured he offered.

Shaun walked down the hall carrying a tray with three cups of coffee on it, and we walked into the room. I piled the pillows on the bed, and we all sat on the love seat. I spoke in hushed tones, explaining my encounter with my other side. They both sat there speechless until I was finished, then they began responding in whispers so as not to wake Krista.

"So, you are a protector, a werewolf, and the void?" Shaun asked.

"I guess that's pretty accurate." I sighed, still confused about the situation.

"Wow, Jai, we need to talk with your grandparents," Corbin said.

"At least now I understand who that voice was speaking through me at the park. That gives me some comfort and answered one of my many questions." My stomach growled loudly, and my cheeks burned in response.

Corbin chuckled. "I think that's my clue to cook breakfast."

All I could do was smile at him in response.

Krista woke, and we all ate breakfast without mention of last night's events. We just enjoyed spending time with each other.

Corbin and I cleaned the kitchen while Shaun took Krista on a tour of the compound. Afterward, we decided to meet up at the Weaver plantation.

I needed to talk to my grandparents, and Krista still needed to have a checkup with the doctor. I was sure she could use some vitamins and perhaps a tetanus shot. Who knew what kind of germs and bacteria were in that filthy place she described?

Mom and Dad were already training in the backyard when we arrived. We went out to explain about the void while Grams took Krista to the clinic.

It was hard to talk with my parents with the urge to constantly hug them. I managed to control the urge, but it wasn't easy. Too much time had been stolen from us. But I needed to make sure the red-eyed demon didn't ruin the remaining time I had with them.

After I finished giving her every detail of my dreams and visions, I said, "Mom, what do you think about the void being part of me?"

"Well, it makes sense. The power displayed in that little cabin the night you were born radiated for miles and miles. It was astonishing and terrifying at the same time."

"I think we need to listen to what the void is telling you," Dad said. His eyes turned the color of mustard. "And we need to begin your training. We should have had this time with you when you were little, but that little rat took that time away from us."

Chapter Twelve

TRAINING 101

"While there are many different training methods used here in the compound, your mother and I tend to do all our training in the garden. Come rain or shine, we'll be out there." Dad gathered supplies to take outside.

"We have very little time, and they'll be searching for you," Mom said. "We need to make sure you're ready if they find you." She laid out several notebooks neatly on a table.

Mom worked on all things element-related while Grams tackled spells and potions. When she was able to leave the hospital.

Dad taught me all things wolf-related. Corbin and Gramps watched and cheered me on. Jonathan chimed in a time or two, giving me suggestions and input where needed.

Working with mom was amazing. She had so much patience with me.

"Jai, honey, concentrate and try again. The water will respond to you if you respect it. Feel the current move through your body." She moved her hands around in a wave-like motion. "Tell the waves what you want them to do. They are yours to command. Allow yourself to relax and let the power grow."

I did as she said. It was incredible! The water flowed through me as if I was the liquid itself. It moved when I willed it to do so. I did it! I had managed to conquer my first power.

The element of Earth was my favorite but probably not much help in a fight. I learned to grow many different flowers and vegetables. I created a seat out of ivy and helped a dying tree blossom bloom.

The element of Wind was a tricky one. I could control the temperature of the wind as well as its force and direction. It was realizing which one was which that was the hard part.

Especially when I felt cold, then the wind's temperature increased to warm me.

"It's all in the motion of your breath," Mom demonstrated as she instructed. "If you want a spiral of wind, roll your tongue and exhale to the strength you need the wind to blow. When you inhale, the wind will settle down. If you exhale, it will get stronger. The temperature will come later once you master the trait itself."

I ran through every exercise and could tell I was getting stronger. I still struggled with it, but I knew I'd figure it out with more practice.

The element of fire was easy to control based on my emotions. If I thought about demons, the flame grew bigger and bigger. To calm the massive fire, I simply thought of Corbin. So, if I could control my thoughts, I'd be great. But if I was irrational, I could burn down the entire state. That one needed a lot more meditation and practice. And I still couldn't manifest it on my own.

By the end of the afternoon, I could control every gift I was given. I even transformed into my wolf form. Corbin stroked my caramel-colored fur and kept giving me hugs until I was forced to turn back to my human form prematurely. I was a little creeped out at being a wolf and having him pet me. Because my thoughts got away from me, I ended up naked in his lap.

"Whoa, umm..." was all I could get out of my mouth before Mom threw a cover over me. I looked up at Corbin and his face was as red as a tomato. I'm not sure which one of us was more embarrassed, but I found his blushing hilarious and busted out laughing. He joined me after a few minutes.

"I think we have mastered a lot for now. Let's take a break and go eat," Gramps suggested.

I was exhausted. I finally understood what the Void meant about how not having much energy would pose a problem. Magic took a lot out of a person. One would think having all this power would make a girl more energetic, not overwhelm her with exhaustion.

"We only have one more day before All Hallows' Eve." How much more was there for me to learn?

"We need to be ready for anything," Corbin said. "Who knows how powerful they are?"

"Let's get the map out and see if we can figure out where to send the scouts. We need to get to that power source." Then I took a bite of my turkey sandwich. After I swallowed, I continued, pointing at the map. "Look, there's an underground railroad about twenty miles from the park. That might be the location we're looking for."

Corbin stood up to take a closer look. "I think you might be right."

"How fast can you get our scouts out there?" Gramps asked.

"I can send them right away." Corbin grabbed his cell phone to make the call.

"Jai, you need to go get some rest. I have a feeling we're in for a long night." Gramps patted my back.

"I'll rest once Krista returns from the clinic."

"Well, don't wait too long. You need your energy," Corbin said. He finished the necessary phone calls, and the scouts were on their way. Then he walked me back to his house and lay beside me while I waited to hear from my grandmother.

"Do you think she's okay?" I asked.

"Don't worry, sweets. I'm sure Mary would have called you otherwise. She most likely was dehydrated and needed fluid infusions. Get some rest. I'll wake you as soon as there's news." He rubbed soft circles on my forearm as I drifted off to sleep.

Chapter Thirteen

OVERCHARGED

"Jai, wake up," Corbin whispered. "There's news from the scouts."

I sat up and rubbed my sleepy eyes. "Is Krista back yet?"

"No. Mary said she's doing fine but needs some vitamins and a lot of rest. She feels its best she stays in the hospital a few days to fully recover. She has also said no guests until this fight is over."

"What? What does she mean, no guests? I'm her best friend and nobody is telling me I can't see her." I jumped out of bed.

"Settle down, Jai. You know Mary wouldn't keep you away unless it was necessary." He wrapped his arm around me in an attempt to calm me down.

I sighed. "Well, can I at least call her?"

"Absolutely, you can." He queued up the number and handed me his cell phone. I quickly snatched it away, eager to hear my friend's voice.

"Hello?" a very quiet voice answered.

"Krista, is that you?"

"Jai, it's you. Where are you?" Her voice perked up.

"I'm at Corbin's. He says I can't visit until you are well. Are you okay? What are they doing to you?" My nerves tingled with worry.

"I'm okay. Mary said I just need a lot of rest. She is taking very good care of me. I'll be fine. She tells me you must go back out tonight. I'm so worried about you being in danger. Please come back to me."

I could tell she was crying.

"I'll come now if you want. They can't keep me away."

"No, it can wait. Just please promise you'll kill that thing then come back and get me." Her voice quivered.

"I promise, Krista. I will see you soon. I love you." I struggled to hold in my tears.

"I love you, too."

I hung up the phone and placed it on the nightstand, then I sat quietly on the side of the bed, trying to hold it together. Everything had finally sunk in, and I felt the weight of the world on my shoulders.

There were many people counting on me. I knew I must be strong and survive, one way or another. I would not let that demon destroy my one chance at happiness.

"Jai, if we are going to get ahead of the game, we need to leave soon," Corbin said.

"I know. I'm ready. I'm just not so sure I can do this."

"I've seen what you're capable of without proper training. And now you have it. I have no doubt in you." He stood in front of me and combed my hair out of my face with his hand. "You can do this, and I will be right there beside you the whole time."

"No, you can't. We didn't get the dagger, and I won't risk losing you." I stood and pressed my face into his chest.

"Jai, have some faith in me. I'm stronger than you think. I'll be careful, but I won't let you do this alone." He pulled me back to look at my face. "In fact, half of the scouts will be with us. The other half will be at the compound should anything go wrong."

"I suppose it's now or never." I pulled my new warrior outfit out of the closet.

Corbin kissed my head and exited the room to allow me to dress.

I took a deep breath and pulled on the same black leather pants, sweater, and black leather jacket from before. I dressed quickly and sat on the stool in front of my bathroom mirror. I pulled up my favorite song on my cell phone and let the music help motivate me. I was ready. I exited the room and met up with the rest of the crew.

We rode out via motorcycles, which scared the crap out of me. But apparently, it was the best way to get in and out unnoticed.

"The scouts are going ahead of us to clear out as many guards as they can before we arrive. If this is the right place, it will be heavily guarded."

I heard fighting up ahead. No turning back now.

Corbin stopped the motorcycle, and we crept up to the entrance of the railway.

A dozen figures cut through the brush, eyes blazing red as fire. It was all struggle, all hell-a flashing, blinding chaos as men scrambled to find cover. Bodies both good and evil fell.

The entrance was dark and appeared to be unkempt. That explained why they decided to make it their hideout for all those years.

Our scouts were doing an excellent job at causing a distraction.

Corbin and I snuck in unnoticed. It smelled of rotting flesh, and the ground was mushy under my feet. I was thankful for the combat boots. My stomach turned as we passed a decaying deer, the scent causing my nose to burn.

"Are you okay?" Corbin whispered in my ear.

"Yeah, just a little unsettled." I swallowed and tried to cover my nose with my jacket collar.

We walked about a mile, not really seeing anything that resembled an entrance. The passage was just a long train tunnel.

"Stop." I threw my arm to halt Corbin. My animal instincts had kicked in. "Do you smell that?"

"No, I don't smell anything."

"I smell something. Iron, maybe." I took a few more steps and peeked around the corner. Two guards picked through the remains of what once was a young lady.

The corpse lay on a table, her bony rib cage torn apart. Frantic fingers clutched and clawed at her mutilated belly as they sampled pieces of her flesh. I lost my footing and fell backward, but Corbin caught me before I made a sound.

Vomit rose in my throat, and I bent over to expel the remains of my last meal. I tried to keep myself quiet as I retched. Corbin held me tight as we listened.

"That's the third one this week," the guard said. His shirt was bloody, and his slimy brown hair was glued to his face with blood.

"How hard is it to find a virgin around here, anyway?" the other guard said. They looked almost identical in appearance.

"Troy is not going to be happy if we don't find him a virgin before the ceremony," Guard One said.

"They don't have all the pieces they need to complete the Harvest," I whispered. Hope began to fill me.

Corbin took out a bow and shot an arrow at one of the men. He fell, causing blood to splatter the other guard in the face. Corbin ran in and stabbed him before he even knew what had happened. As his mouth frothed, he choked on his own blood, gazing ahead in disbelief as he fell to the ground.

"See, I told you, I'm crazy fast." He bounced on the balls of his feet.

"Yeah, yeah. I see. Just don't get yourself killed." I rolled my eyes and mumbled, "Showoff."

The trail of gore led to a bloody room washed in death. Mutilated, decayed bodies were spread throughout. There were no cages there, just blood-filled tables and death. We walked down the dark hallway and listened for any signs of life.

A loud *boom* made me jump. A scream escaped my mouth before I could stop it.

Corbin quickly wrapped his hand around my lips and pulled me back behind a pillar.

"Who is there?" Troy growled.

I'd recognize his voice anywhere. We stayed still, knowing we needed to destroy that energy unit before we attempted to eradicate Troy.

He closed the door with a sharp snap.

Corbin released his hand from my mouth, and I breathed a soft sigh. "Well, at least we know where he is." I whispered. We crept passed the door and made our way farther down the trail. I saw the cages in the distance.

"I think we found it." I spoke a little louder than I wanted. A quick glance around showed no guards. Or anyone else. All the cages were empty.

We walked farther, and I noticed Krista's black high heel shoe in the corner of one of the cages. My heart skipped a beat when I saw the dried blood in the cage.

I tore my gaze from the devastation and continued my search for the energy unit. Corbin felt me tense up and placed his hand on the small of my back, giving me some comfort.

"Look, there are the chairs." Corbin pointed to my left.

It was dark, and I had to strain my eyes to see. "I see them," I whispered. There were a set of twelve chairs in one cage and a set of two in another. All of them had lines running into this massive square box.

It didn't look like what I had expected it to. It was solid black metal that reached all the way to the ceiling. There were no buttons or lights on it indicating how to shut it down. We walked closer, and the lights in the room sprang to action, causing us to turn around quickly.

Troy stood behind us, smiling, a hungry look of satisfaction on his face. "I knew you would come running back for vengeance, little wolf."

"You're mistaken. I'm not here for vengeance." My inner wolf was clawing to come out. "I'm here to put an end to you, once and for all."

I stepped backward, hoping to get closer to the energy unit. There were about twenty steps between me and the monster.

Corbin turned and ran toward the unit.

I exhaled, throwing a blast of wind toward Troy. It caught him off guard, but he didn't budge from his position.

"You're going to have try harder than that, child." He laughed, satisfied to show his strength.

I heard Corbin messing around behind me, trying to figure out how to release the energy built up in the unit. To give him time, I continued to taunt Troy. "Why do you want to open this stupid portal, anyway?"

"Why do you think, little wolf?" He snarled, revealing his razor-sharp teeth at me.

"I haven't the slightest clue, Troy. Or should I call you traitor?" I asked in a sarcastic voice.

"I don't really care what you call me." He walked closer to me. "Don't worry, little wolf, you and your little boyfriend will be side by side very soon." He took another step toward me. "I will drain you both together, you see. I don't need that pesky little amulet now that I have you."

Beads of sweat formed on my forehead, and my body tensed. I did all I could to control my inner wolf, but it was growing restless. I looked around the room to see if there was anything I could use to defend myself other than magic. I understood the importance of reserving my energy, now more than ever. I allowed my inner wolf to emerge enough to jump at him.

He knocked me down in midair. I fell to the ground with a thud. A loud *snap* sounded as a bone cracked in my ankle. The pain radiated up my leg, but I managed to push it out of my mind. I had to get up.

His laughing made my blood boil. I played off my injury as he walked closer. He knelt beside me, so close I could feel his hot, foul breath on my face.

"Stop trying so hard, little wolf. There was never a chance of you defeating me." He sniffed. "Ah, I can smell your delicious essence."

Catching him off guard, I elbowed him in the face, causing him to lose balance. Then, I kicked him over and over. He lay there, laughing at me as though my attack didn't faze him.

That only made me angrier.

"Jai, don't lose control! It's what he wants!" Corbin yelled.

I inhaled a quick breath and exhaled, using the power of wind to push him further away from me.

"Any luck back there, Corbin?" I shouted.

"I found a lever. I just can't get it to release."

"Hurry. I can't hold him back for too long."

"You will never be able to shut down that machine," Troy gloated as he walked toward me. He jumped at me, knocking me down.

I crawled backward quickly, and my hand stumbled upon a large piece of broken concrete. I held on to it as I waited for him to approach me.

His hungry eyes never left mine. He growled and jumped toward me. I screamed and swung with all my might, hitting him with the concrete. It crunched his skull, leaving a bloody knot on his head.

I tried to reserve as much energy as I could, but I realized the Void was right. It would take both of us to bring him down. I looked around for anything else I could use. No fire, no water... but I had earth. I quickly ran toward Corban. I closed off my mind and concentrated on the ground. It began to shake. I stepped back and grabbed Corbin's hand.

"Count to ten, then torch that machine with all you have," I said. "I'll join in once I get this creep out of here." I waved my hand and stomped my foot. The ground vibrated and started to crumble between Troy and me.

"You think that will stop me?" He grabbed my hand, pulling me away from Corbin.

I wrestled my way out of his arms and crab-walked backward quickly to create some space between us. The earth crumbled more and opened between us. The open grave gaped wide, ready to receive him. I felt heat behind me, letting me know Corbin had started the fire. I released my restraint and allowed the earth to collapse beneath Troy and swallow him up.

A cold light of fear shone in his eyes as he struggled to climb out of the broken earth.

I jumped, calling on my animal instincts, and landed close to Corbin as the ground closed, trapping Troy underground in the process.

"We have to hurry. That hole won't hold him long." The heat of the fire surrounded me. I began to focus on the fire Corbin had started and used my gift to make it grow and get hotter. The smoldering metal curled up around the edges. If we could keep it up, it might just break.

"Wait, Jai. What happens when something hot is hit with freezing temperatures?" Corbin said.

Wonderful idea. "I don't know if I can do it, but I'll try." I inhaled and let the fire get close to me. As my skin started to burn, I began to exhale freezing wind, causing a blizzard of metal to explode around us.

The next thing I knew, I was hit with a blast of light. I flew backward, hitting my head hard on one of the cage doors.

Shards of metal were embedded in my skin. Warm sticky blood flowed down my face.

I was so close. I would not give up.

"We did it!" Corbin ran to me. He lifted me, revealing the shattered pieces of what used to be a powerful energy force. The wall behind it disintegrated from the explosion, leaving a gaping hole through which moonlight shone in.

"What did you do?" Troy dug his way out of the earth. His eyes glowed a deep crimson.

"We've taken what's precious to you." I laughed. I grew dizzy, either from the blood-gushing wound on my forehead or from the amount of energy I'd used. But I didn't care. It was time to end it. "It's time, Void. Do your worst!" Her intense power grew inside me, and I willingly allowed her to emerge within me.

"You will not have the satisfaction of harming this innocent any longer!" we bellowed. Her voice was chilling and full of anger as she swerved her neck in a snake like motion.

"You think you can challenge me?" Troy shouted as he walked closer. His gaze was hollow, his eyes cruel and dead.

"You are no match for me." We raised our hand in the air. The wind picked up and the roof began to fall in pieces around us. Our vision clouded with dust. I could barely see what was happening, but I still gave Void all control.

I suppose that's what she meant when she said we were more powerful together.

Corbin ran and grabbed the dagger from Troy. Punch after punch, blow after blow, the men fought on. They wrestled, and I thought Troy had managed to stab Corbin at one point, but he was much faster than the demon and knocked the dagger away. Then he managed to pin Troy and hold him down on the ground.

"Stop!" we yelled, then we pushed Corbin away from Troy with one finger-swipe of air. "Let the Dimension of the Dead swallow you whole, never to return to the land of the living." A funnel began to form in the sky, causing the wind to blow fiercely around us.

We opened our mouth and blew enough breath to push Troy into the air. We watched as he screamed, and his withering body was sucked into the spiral. Once the sky absorbed him, it returned to normal, allowing the stars to calm the storm within my soul.

Then, I blacked out.

Chapter Fourteen

The Harvest

I woke in the hospital, listening to a heart monitor beep.

Corbin slept in a chair beside my bed, his face covered in stubble from lack of shaving. He looked exhausted. I must have been out for days.

I sat up, looked around, and pulled the covers off me. I suppose there was some sort of alarm underneath me to alert the nursing staff I was attempting to get out of bed, because once I moved, an annoying buzzer repeatedly sounded.

I could defeat a bloodthirsty demon, but I couldn't get out of bed on my own. Ridiculous. I rolled my eyes.

I was thrilled when it wasn't nursing staff that ran to my aid. It was Krista. She had been in the tiny bathroom beside my bed.

She looked radiant in a midnight blue sweater dress. Her hair was pulled up in a loose bun. Her bruises were gone, leaving her skin with its normal beautiful glow. She hugged me so tightly, I thought she was going to crack my rib.

"I knew you would come back. You're too stubborn to die." She laughed.

Corbin also woke after hearing the annoying bed buzzer. He stood and rushed over to me. "Good morning, beautiful." He gazed into my eyes, and I could not look away. I reached for him, our lips meeting each other's. I didn't want to let go. I was completely consumed by him. He was the one who finally pulled away. He had a huge smile across his face, allowing me to see how happy he truly was. "Looks like we have a harvest to celebrate." Then he ran off yelling, "She's awake. She's awake!" And he skipped into the hallway.

"I guess we do." I laughed.

Krista sat on the side of the bed with me and took my hand. "There's something very important I need to talk to you about, but your parents and grandparents are anxiously waiting outside. I'll be back after they leave." She kissed me on the cheek and left the room.

My parents walked in looking refreshed and fully healed.

"Wow! You guys look fantastic." I said, and they both gave me a hug.

"How did you do it?" Mom asked.

"I can't take the credit for Troy. That was my trusty inner Void, but Corbin and I totally destroyed that energy sucker!" Pride tinged my voice.

"We knew when you did, too. We felt it. All our energy was restored instantly," Dad said.

"You two make a pretty good team." Mom elbowed me and grinned.

"Kind of reminds me of the two of us in our younger days, doesn't it Robbie?" He winked at her.

"Stop calling me that, Jimbo!"

It was so good to see them playing and joking with one another. It still felt surreal seeing my parents alive and happy after all these years of waiting.

"We never doubted you." Mom hugged me.

"Your grandparents are patiently waiting outside to see you. Besides, we have a party in your honor to plan." Dad hugged me, and they exited the room.

My grandparents walked in holding a pot full of orange and yellow mums.

"Hello, dear. I thought you might enjoy a little color to your room." Grams placed the flower pot on the window seal and removed the old one and threw it into the trash can.

"How are you feeling?" Gramps asked.

"I'm okay, weak, but I think I'm ready to get out of this bed."

"Well, the good doc says you can get up and out of here once that infusion stops." He pointed to the IV pole. I didn't even realize I was getting an infusion.

"You have been asleep for a while, dear. You required nutrients and a blood transfusion. They had to shave some of your hair, but it isn't bad. Most of that has grown back already." Grams ran her fingers through my hair.

"What? I had no idea." I reached up to feel my head. I didn't feel any bald spot or stitches. My ankle wasn't in a cast, either, but I was certain I had broken it.

"Well, of course you didn't, silly. You were unconscious," the nurse said as she entered the room to check my vitals. I recognized her as the blonde woman I met when I first visited the compound. She looked way more chipper than I remember her to be.

"We all owe you a great deal of thanks," Bethann said as she unplugged the bed monitor. "You saved my boyfriend, Zane, when you brought all those scouts home. I can't say thank you enough for what you did. Also, I'm sorry for how I treated you before. Not one woman in this compound has been able to snag Corbin. I wondered what you had that I didn't, and I was jealous." She blushed.

"I didn't do it alone and you are forgiven." I said as I smiled up at her.

"We are aware of that, dear," Grams chimed in.

"That's why we're planning a celebration for everyone in the compound," Gramps said. "We all worked as a team and proved how strong we are when we stick together."

"Speaking of celebration, we better get to cooking." Grams picked up the phone to dial a number. "Alan, she is awake. We need to get your kitchen stocked. Yes, yes, I'm on my way." She hung up the phone.

"Goodbye, dear. We'll see you soon." She gave me a kiss on the top of my head.

Krista and her mother, Jane, entered as they left the room holding a newborn baby wrapped in a pale pink blanket.

"Jai, I want you to meet Alexandria." She handed me over the beautiful baby girl.

I was confused as to when Jane found out about the compound, but more so about the sweet baby in her arms.

"She is just precious, but who does she belong to?" I felt oddly curious as to why she brought me a baby.

"Me." A large smile spread across her face.

"Wait, what? When did you have a baby? How is that even possible?" Then I paused. "How long was I out?"

"You were out for exactly a year to the day." She said as she pointed to a calendar on the wall.

"What? I lost an entire year?" I whispered. My heart sank, a bubble swelled in my throat, and my eyes filled with tears. "What happened to me?"

"The doctors weren't really certain. You had some minor swelling on your brain, but not enough to cause permanent damage. The only thing they could come up with was you just lost too much energy and your body needed the time to refuel."

"You were in a complete coma. We weren't sure if you would wake up or not. We just watched, waited, and hoped. Corbin only left your side long enough to shower and eat. We all visited several times a day. It was just luck that you woke up during our visit."

I tried to listen to her words, but my mind was full of questions. "Who is her daddy?" My voice cracked. I missed one of the most important days in my friend's life.

"Shaun. Why are you so sad?" She patted my back.

"Why am I sad? Because I missed your pregnancy. I missed her birth." Warm tears ran down my face. Alexandria's little blue eyes looked up at me, and I planted a kiss on her tiny sweet hand.

"She is absolutely incredible." I sobbed, unable to take my eyes off her.

"Momma Jane, I am so sorry I lied to you. I just didn't know what to tell you." I couldn't look her in the eyes.

"All is good. I am quite fond of my grandbaby." She smiled at me. "It's because of you that we have her." She attempted to comfort me.

"She is so perfect, Krista." I kissed her again and took in the scent of baby lotion.

"You'll be glad to know you're her godmother. I also named her after you. Alexandria Jai," Krista said, with a great big smile on her face.

"Wow, I'm a god-mommy." I felt so proud. Tears flowed from my eyes again. My heart overflowed with emotion, just when I thought I couldn't hold anymore.

A soft knock on the door broke our attention. Corbin walked in holding a bouquet of flowers.

"We'll leave you two alone for a moment." Krista winked at Corbin.

I placed a kiss on Alexandria's forehead, gave her back to Krista, and gave my friend and her mom a hug. Then they left us alone.

Corbin knelt beside the bed and kissed my foot. I laughed and dried the tears off my face with the back of my hand. He had gone home, showered, and shaved. I could smell his aftershave. It brought back memories of the night I first saw him in that dance club.

He looked up at me. "Jai, you give me more strength, courage, and joy in a single glance than I have ever deserved or thought possible. I've sat here watching and waiting for this day for twelve long months.

"Dreaming of the day you would be mine again. I knew you would wake up. You have so much love and life left in you. I thank the heavens above for the day I found you. I have thought about what I would say to you when you woke up over and over. That day is finally here, and I cannot stand another moment without you. Jaime Grace Weaver, will you move in with me?" A wide smile lit up his face.

My eyes filled with water once again. My heart almost leapt out of my chest. "Yes! Of course, I'll move in with you. I have loved you from the moment I laid eyes on you."

He jumped up, and I stood beside him. He opened a small brown leather drawstring bag and pulled out a silver key that was attached to my long necklace with my post office key. I knelt my head for him to place the chain around my neck. Then our lips met once again.

My core heated up as my body molded to his. It was short-lived, though. The next thing I knew, everyone was running in the room and offering their congratulations.

I had a lot to be thankful for. I had lost a lot, that was true, but what I gained was far greater than I could have ever imagined.

I had only one request before we attended the harvest celebration. I needed to visit Jonathan's grave.

Corbin and I went alone, stopping at a flower trailer on the way. I picked out a pot of orange mums that matched Jonathan's old brown suit. It made me laugh to think about the day we met. I was terrified of him once I found out he was a ghost. Now, I missed him and his funny laugh. I placed the orange mums by his old and crumbling gravestone.

"Thank you for your help, Uncle Jonathan. You will always be in my heart." I knelt beside his grave. He had told me once that he was only sent when trouble was brewing.

"I have a feeling we'll see you again one-day, old friend. Until we meet again." I kissed my fingers and touched the top of his gravestone.

Then we headed to the celebration and had a grand time being perfectly normal.

ACKNOWLEDGEMENTS

There are so many of you that helped me along the way. I can never say thank you enough.

My sister, Krystal Cornish, who enjoyed my every rewrite and gave me encouragement.

My favorite author and twin at heart, AJ Myers, who gave me pointers, advice and encouragement. As well as making me laugh as I went through my revisions. It is because of you that I found my love for writing.

My closest friends, Sheila Myers, Nancy Stough, for always listening to me talk about writing and reading all my rough drafts.

My launch team, for taking the time to read and give me suggestions.

Chandler Bolt and Self-Publishing School, for teaching me every step of the way.

Jackson Dean Chase and Derek Murphy for publishing awesome books and tutorials for authors. You both helped me make this book possible.

And last, but not least, everyone that has taking time to read my book. My heart is filled with love and appreciation for each one of you.

ABOUT THE AUTHOR

Terrica Simmons was raised in a small town in Arkansas. She has one brother, Jamie Seaborn, and three sisters, Krystal Cornish, Cassie Krupnow and Terri Seaborn.

She attended Crowley's Ridge College then Arkansas State University to obtain a degree in physical therapy. She currently works in a pediatric clinic in the delta and lives in Mississippi.

In her free time, she enjoys watching her kids play baseball, cheer, dance and attends their band concerts.

She enjoys helping others through community service and offering any words of wisdom along the way. She is married to Logan Simmons and has three amazing children, two crazy cats and the sweetest dog.

Did you enjoy the book?

I'd love to hear what you thought about it! Please leave a review for me on Amazon.

www.ingramcontent.com/pod-product-compliance
Lightning Source LLC
Chambersburg PA
CBHW060920250626
47159CB00008B/3098